Andrew Lang

His poems

Andrew Lang

His poems

ISBN/EAN: 9783337282363

Printed in Europe, USA, Canada, Australia, Japan

Cover: Foto ©Andreas Hilbeck / pixelio.de

More available books at **www.hansebooks.com**

ROBERT F. MURRAY

(AUTHOR OF THE SCARLET GOWN)

HIS POEMS: WITH A MEMOIR

BY

ANDREW LANG

LONDON

LONGMANS, GREEN, AND CO.

NEW YORK : 15 EAST 16TH STREET

1894

CONTENTS

R. F. MURRAY

1863-1893

MUCH is written about success and failure in the
career of literature, about the reasons which enable
one man to reach the front, and another to earn his
livelihood, while a third, in appearance as likely as
either of them, fails and, perhaps, faints by the way.
Mr. R. F. Murray, the author of *The Scarlet Gown*,
was among those who do not attain success, in spite
of qualities which seem destined to ensure it, and
who fall out of the ranks. To him, indeed, success
and the rewards of this world, money, and praise,
did by no means seem things to be snatched at.
To him success meant earning by his pen the very
modest sum which sufficed for his wants, and the
leisure necessary for serious essays in poetry. Fate

b

denied him even this, in spite of his charming
natural endowment of humour, of tenderness, of
delight in good letters, and in nature. He died
young; he was one of those whose talent matures
slowly, and he died before he came into the full
possession of his intellectual kingdom. He had the
ambition to excel, αἰὲν ἀριστεύειν, as the Homeric
motto of his University runs, and he was on the way
to excellence when his health broke down. He
lingered for two years and passed away.

It is a familiar story, the story of lettered youth;
of an ambition, or rather of an ideal; of poverty;
of struggles in the 'dusty and stony ways'; of
intellectual task-work; of a true love consoling the
last months of weakness and pain. The tale is
not repeated here because it is novel, nor even
because in its hero we have to regret an 'inheritor
of unfulfilled renown.' It is not the genius so
much as the character of this St. Andrews student
which has won the sympathy of his biographer,
and may win, he hopes, the sympathy of others.
In Mr. Murray I feel that I have lost that rare

thing, a friend; a friend whom the chances of life threw in my way, and withdrew again ere we had time and opportunity for perfect recognition. Those who read his Letters and Remains may also feel this emotion of sympathy and regret.

He was young in years, and younger in heart, a lover of youth; and youth, if it could learn and could be warned, might win a lesson from his life. Many of us have trod in his path, and, by some kindness of fate, have found from it a sunnier exit into longer days and more fortunate conditions. Others have followed this well-beaten road to the same early and quiet end as his.

The life and the letters of Murray remind one strongly of Thomas Davidson's, as published in that admirable and touching biography, *A Scottish Probationer*. It was my own chance to be almost in touch with both these gentle, tuneful, and kindly humorists. Davidson was a Borderer, born on the skirts of 'stormy Ruberslaw,' in the country of James Thomson, of Leyden, of the old Ballad minstrels. The son of a Scottish peasant line of the old sort, honourable, refined, devout, he was educated in Edinburgh for the ministry of the United Presbyterian Church. Some beautiful verses of his appeared in the *St. Andrews University Magazine* about 1863, at the time when I first 'saw myself in print' in the same periodical. Davidson's poem delighted me: another of his, 'Ariadne in Naxos,' appeared in the *Cornhill Magazine* about the same time. Mr. Thackeray, who was then editor, no doubt remembered Pen's prize poem on the same subject. I did not succeed in learning anything about the author, did not know that he lived within a drive of my own home. When next I heard of him, it was in his biography. As a 'Probationer,' or unplaced minister, he, somehow, was not successful. A humorist, a poet, a delightful companion, he never became 'a placed minister.' It was the old story of an imprudence, a journey made in damp clothes, of consumption, of the end of his earthly life and love. His letters to his betrothed, his poems, his career, constantly remind one of Murray's, who must often have joined in singing Davidson's song, so popular with St. Andrews students, *The Banks of the Yang-tse-kiang.* Love of the Border, love of Murray's 'dear St. Andrews Bay,' love of letters, make one akin to both of these friends who were lost before their friendship was won. Why did not Murray succeed to the measure of his most modest desire? If we examine the records of literary success, we find it won, in the highest fields, by what, for want of a better word, we call genius; in the lower paths, by an energy which can take pleasure in all and every exercise of pen and ink, and can communicate its pleasure to others. Now for Murray one does not venture, in face of his still not wholly developed talent, and of his checked career, to claim genius. He was not a Keats, a Burns, a Shelley: he was not, if one may choose modern examples, a Kipling or a Stevenson. On the other hand, his was a high ideal; he believed, with André Chénier, that he had 'something there,' something worthy of reverence and of careful training within him. Consequently, as we shall see, the drudgery of the pressman was

excessively repulsive to him. He could take no
delight in making the best of it. We learn that
Mr. Kipling's early tales were written as part of
hard daily journalistic work in India ; written in
torrid newspaper offices, to fill columns. Yet they
were written with the delight of the artist, and are
masterpieces in their *genre.* Murray could not
make the best of ordinary pen-work in this manner.
Again, he was incapable of 'transactions,' of com-
promises ; most honourably incapable of earning
his bread by agreeing, or seeming to agree with
opinions which were not his. He could not endure
(here I think he was wrong) to have his pieces of
light and mirthful verse touched in any way by
an editor. Even where no opinions were concerned,
even where an editor has (to my mind) a perfect
right to alter anonymous contributions, Murray
declined to be edited. I ventured to remonstrate
with him, to say *non est tanti*, but I spoke too late,
or spoke in vain. He carried independence too far,
or carried it into the wrong field, for a piece of
humorous verse, say in *Punch*, is not an original

masterpiece and immaculate work of art, but more
or less of a joint-stock product between the editor,
the author, and the public. Macaulay, and Carlyle,
and Sir Walter Scott suffered editors gladly or with
indifference, and who are we that we should complain ? This extreme sensitiveness would always
have stood in Murray's way.

Once more, Murray's interest in letters was much
more energetic than his zeal in the ordinary industry
of a student. As a general rule, men of original
literary bent are not exemplary students at college.
'The common curricoolum,' as the Scottish laird
called academic studies generally, rather repels
them. Macaulay took no honours at Cambridge ;
mathematics defied him. Scott was 'the Greek
dunce,' at Edinburgh. Thackeray, Shelley, Gibbon,
did not cover themselves with college laurels ;
they read what pleased them, they did not read
'for the schools.' In short, this behaviour at
college is the rule among men who are to be distinguished in literature, not the exception. The
honours attained at Oxford by Mr. Swinburne, whose

Greek verses are no less poetical than his English poetry, were inconspicuous. At St. Andrews, Murray read only 'for human pleasure,' like Scott, Thackeray, Shelley, and the rest, at Edinburgh, Oxford, and Cambridge. In this matter, I think, he made an error, and one which affected his whole career. He was not a man of private fortune, like some of those whom we have mentioned. He had not a business ready for him to step into. He had to force his own way in life, had to make himself 'self-supporting.' This was all the more essential to a man of his honourable independence of character, a man who not only would not ask a favour, but who actually shrunk back from such chances as were offered to him, if these chances seemed to be connected with the least discernible shadow of an obligation. At St. Andrews, had he chosen to work hard in certain branches of study, he might probably have gained an exhibition, gone to Oxford or elsewhere, and, by winning a fellowship, secured the leisure which was necessary for the development of his powers. I confess to believing

in strenuous work at the classics, as offering,
apart from all material reward, the best and most
solid basis, especially where there is no exuberant
original genius, for the career of a man of letters.
The mental discipline is invaluable, the training in
accuracy is invaluable, and invaluable is the life led
in the society of the greatest minds, the noblest
poets, the most faultless artists of the world. To
descend to ordinary truths, scholarship is, at lowest,
an honourable *gagne-pain*. But Murray, like the
majority of students endowed with literary originality,
did not share these rather old-fashioned ideas. The
clever Scottish student is apt to work only too hard,
and, perhaps, is frequently in danger of exhausting
his powers before they are mature, and of injuring
his health before it is confirmed. His ambitions, to
lookers-on, may seem narrow and school-boyish, as
if he were merely emulous, and eager for a high
place in his 'class,' as lectures are called in Scotland.
This was Murray's own view, and he certainly
avoided the dangers of academic over-work. He
read abundantly, but, as Fitzgerald says, he read

'for human pleasure.' He never was a Greek scholar, he disliked Philosophy, as presented to him in class-work; the gods had made him poetical, not metaphysical.

There was one other cause of his lack of even such slender commercial success in letters as was really necessary to a man who liked 'plain living and high thinking.' He fell early in love with a city, with a place—he lost his heart to St. Andrews. Here, at all events, his critic can sympathise with him. His 'dear St. Andrews Bay,' beautiful alike in winter mists and in the crystal days of still winter sunshine; the quiet brown streets brightened by the scarlet gowns; the long limitless sands; the dark blue distant hills, and far-off snowy peaks of the Grampians; the majestic melancholy towers, monuments of old religion overthrown; the deep dusky porch of the college chapel, with Kennedy's arms in wrought iron on the oaken door; the solid houses with their crow steps and gables, all the forlorn memories of civil and religious feud, of inhabitants saintly, royal, heroic, endeared St.

Andrews to Murray. He could not say, like our
other poet to Oxford, 'Farewell, dear city of youth
and dream!' His whole nature needed the air,
'like wine.' He found, as he remarks, 'health and
happiness in the German Ocean,' swimming out
beyond the 'lake' where the witches were dipped;
walking to the grey little coast-towns, with their
wealth of historic documents, their ancient kirks and
graves; dreaming in the vernal woods of Mount
Melville or Strathtyrum; rambling (without a fish-
ing-rod) in the charmed 'dens' of the Kenley burn,
a place like Tempe in miniature: these things were
Murray's usual enjoyments, and they became his
indispensable needs. His peculiarly shy and, as it
were, silvan nature, made it physically impossible for
him to live in crowded streets and push his way
through throngs of indifferent men. He could not
live even in Edinburgh; he made the effort, and his
health, at no time strong, seems never to have
recovered from the effects of a few months spent
under a roof in a large town. He hurried back to
St. Andrews: her fascination was too powerful.

Hence it is that, dying with his work scarcely begun, he will always be best remembered as the poet of *The Scarlet Gown*, the Calverley or J. K. S. of Kilrymont; endowed with their humour, their skill in parody, their love of youth, but (if I am not prejudiced) with more than the tenderness and natural magic of these regretted writers. Not to be able to endure crowds and towns, (a matter of physical health and constitution, as well as of temperament) was, of course, fatal to an ordinary success in journalism. On the other hand, Murray's name is inseparably connected with the life of youth in the little old college, in the University of the Admirable Crichton and Claverhouse, of the great Montrose and of Ferguson,—the harmless Villon of Scotland,—the University of almost all the famous Covenanters, and of all the valiant poet-Cavaliers. Murray has sung of the life and pleasures of its students, of examinations and *Gaudeamuses*—supper parties—he has sung of the sands, the links, the sea, the towers, and his name and fame are for ever blended with the air of his city of youth and dream.

It is not a wide name or a great fame, but it is what he would have desired, and we trust that it may be long-lived and enduring. We are not to wax elegiac, and adopt a tearful tone over one so gallant and so uncomplaining. He failed, but he was undefeated.

In the following sketch of Murray's life and work use is made of his letters, chiefly of letters to his mother. They always illustrate his own ideas and attempts; frequently they throw the light of an impartial and critical mind on the distinguished people whom Murray observed from without. It is worth remarking that among many remarks on persons, I have found not one of a censorious, cynical, envious, or unfriendly nature. Youth is often captious and keenly critical; partly because youth generally has an ideal, partly, perhaps chiefly, from mere intellectual high spirits and sense of the incongruous; occasionally the motive is jealousy or spite. Murray's sense of fun was keen, his ideal was lofty; of envy, of an injured sense of being neglected, he does not show one trace. To make fun of their masters and pastors, tutors, professors, is the general and not necessarily unkind tendency of pupils. Murray rarely mentions any of the professors in St. Andrews except in terms of praise, which is often enthusiastic. Now, as he was by no means a prize student, or pattern young man for a story-book, this generosity is a high proof of an admirable nature. If he chances to speak to his mother about a bore, and he did not suffer bores gladly, he not only does not name the person, but gives no hint by which he might be identified. He had much to embitter him, for he had a keen consciousness of 'the something within him,' of the powers which never found full expression; and he saw others advancing and prospering while he seemed to be standing still, or losing ground in all ways. But no word of bitterness ever escapes him in the correspondence which I have seen. In one case he has to speak of a disagreeable and disappointing interview with a man from whom he had been led to expect sympathy and encouragement. He told me about this affair in conversation; 'There

were tears in my eyes as I turned from the house,'
he said, and he was not effusive. In a letter to
Mrs. Murray he describes this unlucky interview,—
a discouragement caused by a manner which was
strange to Murray, rather than by real unkindness,
—and he describes it with a delicacy, with a reserve,
with a toleration, beyond all praise. These are
traits of a character which was greater and more
rare than his literary talent: a character quite
developed, while his talent was only beginning
to unfold itself, and to justify his belief in his
powers.

Robert Murray was the eldest child of John and
Emmeline Murray : the father a Scot, the mother
of American birth. He was born at Roxbury, in
Massachusetts, on December 26th, 1863. It may
be fancy, but, in his shy reserve, his almost *farouche*
independence, one seems to recognise the Scot ;
while in his cast of literary talent, in his natural
'culture,' we observe the son of a refined American
lady. To his mother he could always write about
the books which were interesting him, with full

reliance on her sympathy, though indeed, he does not often say very much about literature.

Till 1869 he lived in various parts of New England, his father being a Unitarian minister. 'He was a remarkably cheerful and affectionate child, and seldom seemed to find anything to trouble him.' In 1869 his father carried him to England, Mrs. Murray and a child remaining in America. For more than a year the boy lived with kinsfolk near Kelso, the beautiful old town on the Tweed where Scott passed some of his childish days. In 1871 the family were reunited at York, where he was fond of attending the services in the Cathedral. Mr. Murray then took charge of the small Unitarian chapel of Blackfriars, at Canterbury. Thus Murray's early youth was passed in the mingled influences of Unitarianism at home, and of Cathedral services at York, and in the church where Becket suffered martyrdom. A not unnatural result was a somewhat eclectic and unconstrained religion. He thought but little of the differences of creed, believing that all good men held, in essentials, much the same faith. His view of essentials was generous, as he admitted. He occasionally spoke of himself as 'sceptical,' that is, in contrast with those whose faith was more definite, more dogmatic, more securely based on 'articles.' To illustrate Murray's religious attitude, at least as it was in 1887, one may quote from a letter of that year (April 17).

'There was a University sermon, and I thought I would go and hear it. So I donned my old cap and gown and felt quite proud of them. The preacher was Bishop Wordsworth. He goes in for the union of the Presbyterian and Episcopalian Churches, and is glad to preach in a Presbyterian Church, as he did this morning. How the aforesaid Union is to be brought about, I'm sure I don't know, for I am pretty certain that the Episcopalians won't give up their bishops, and the Presbyterians won't have them on any account. However, that's neither here nor there—at least it does not affect the fact that Wordsworth is a first-rate man, and a fine preacher. I dare say you know he is a nephew or grand-nephew of the Poet. He is a most venerable old man, and worth looking at, merely for his exterior. He is so feeble with age that he can with difficulty climb the three short steps that lead into the pulpit; but, once in the pulpit, it is another thing. There is no feebleness

when he begins to preach. He is one of the last voices
of the old orthodox school, and I wish there were
hundreds like him. If ever a man believed in his mess-
age, Wordsworth does. And though I cannot follow
him in his veneration for the Thirty-nine Articles, the
way in which he does makes me half wish I could. . . .
It was full of wisdom and the beauty of holiness, which
even I, poor sceptic and outcast, could recognise and
appreciate. After all, he didn't get it from the Articles,
but from his own human heart, which, he told us, was
deceitful and desperately wicked.

'Confound it, how stupid we all are ! Episcopalians,
Presbyterians, Unitarians, Agnostics ; the whole lot of
us. We all believe the same things, to a great extent ;
but we must keep wrangling about the data from which
we infer these beliefs. . . . I believe a great deal that
he does, but I certainly don't act up to my belief as he
does to his.'

The belief 'up to' which Murray lived was, if
it may be judged by its fruits, that of a Christian
man. But, in this age, we do find the most exemplary Christian conduct in some who have dis-
carded dogma and resigned hope. Probably Murray
would not the less have regarded these persons as
Christians. If we must make a choice, it is better

to have love and charity without belief, than belief
of the most intense kind, accompanied by such love
and charity as John Knox bore to all who differed
from him about a mass or a chasuble, a priest or
a presbyter. This letter, illustrative of the effect
of cathedral services on a young Unitarian, is taken
out of its proper chronological place.

From Canterbury Mr. Murray went to Ilminster
in Somerset. Here Robert attended the Grammar
School; in 1879 he went to the Grammar School
of Crewkerne. In 1881 he entered at the University of St. Andrews, with a scholarship won as
an external student of Manchester New College.
This he resigned not long after, as he had abandoned
the idea of becoming a Unitarian minister.

No longer a schoolboy, he was now a *Bejant*
(*bec jaune*?), to use the old Scotch term for 'freshman.' He liked the picturesque word, and opposed
the introduction of 'freshman.' Indeed he liked
all things old, and, as a senior man, was a supporter
of ancient customs and of *esprit de corps* in college.
He fell in love for life with that old and grey

enchantress, the city of St. Margaret, of Cardinal Beaton, of Knox and Andrew Melville, of Archbishop Sharp, and Samuel Rutherford. The nature of life and education in a Scottish university is now, probably, better understood in England than it used to be. Of the Scottish universities, St. Andrews varies least, though it varies much, from Oxford and Cambridge. Unlike the others, Aberdeen, Glasgow, and Edinburgh, the United College of St. Leonard and St. Salvator is not lost in a large town. The College and the Divinity Hall of St. Mary's are a survival from the Middle Ages. The University itself arose from a voluntary association of the learned in 1410. Privileges were conferred on this association by Bishop Wardlaw in 1411. It was intended as a bulwark against Lollard ideas. In 1413 the Antipope Benedict XIII., to whom Scotland then adhered, granted six bulls of confirmation to the new University. Not till 1430 did Bishop Wardlaw give a building in South Street, the Pædagogium. St. Salvator's College was founded by Bishop Kennedy (1440-1466): it was confirmed by Pius II. in 1458. Kennedy endowed his foundation richly with plate (a silver mace is still extant) and with gorgeous furniture and cloth of gold. St. Leonard's was founded by Prior Hepburn in 1512. Of St. Salvator's the ancient chapel still remains, and is in use. St. Leonard's was merged with St. Salvator's in the last century: its chapel is now roofless, some of the old buildings remain, much modernised, but on the south side fronting the gardens they are still picturesque. Both Colleges were, originally, places of residence for the students, as at Oxford and Cambridge, and the discipline, especially at St. Leonard's, was rather monastic. The Reformation caused violent changes; all through these troubled ages the new doctrines, and then the violent Presbyterian pretensions to clerical influence in politics, and the Covenant and the Restoration and Revolution, kept busy the dwellers in what should have been 'quiet collegiate cloisters.' St. Leonard's was more extreme, on Knox's side, than St. Salvator's, but was also more devoted to King James in 1715.

From St. Andrews Simon Lovat went to lead his abominable old father's clan, on the Prince Regent's side, in 1745. Golf and archery, since the Reformation at least, were the chief recreations of the students, and the archery medals bear all the noblest names of the North, including those of Argyll and the great Marquis of Montrose. Early in the present century the old ruinous college buildings of St. Salvator's ceased to be habitable, except by a ghost! There is another spectre of a noisy sort in St. Leonard's. The new buildings are mere sets of class-rooms, the students live where they please, generally in lodgings, which they modestly call *bunks*. There is a hall for dinners in common; it is part of the buildings of the Union, a new hall added to an ancient house.

It was thus to a university with ancient associations, with a *religio loci*, and with more united and harmonious student-life than is customary in Scotland, that Murray came in 1881. How clearly his biographer remembers coming to the same place, twenty years earlier! how vivid is his memory of

quaint streets, grey towers, and the North Sea breaking in heavy rollers on the little pier !

Though, like a descendant of Archbishop Sharp,
and a winner of the archery medal, I boast myself
Sancti Leonardi alumnus addictissimus, I am unable
to give a description, at first hand, of student life
in St. Andrews.   In my time, a small set of 'men'
lived together in what was then St. Leonard's Hall.
The buildings that remain on the site of Prior
Hepburn's foundation, or some of them, were turned
into a hall, where we lived together, not scattered
in *bunks*. The existence was mainly like that of
pupils of a private tutor; seven-eighths of private
tutor to one-eighth of a college in the English universities. We attended the lectures in the University, we
distinguished ourselves no more than Murray would
have approved of, and many of us have remained
united by friendship through half a lifetime.

It was a pleasant existence, and the perfume of
buds and flowers in the old gardens, hard by those
where John Knox sat and talked with James Melville and our other predecessors at St. Leonard's,

is fragrant in our memories. It was pleasant, but
St. Leonard's Hall has ceased to be, and the life
there was not the life of the free and hardy bunk-
dwellers. Whoso pined for such dissipated pleasures
as the chill and dark streets of St. Andrews offer to
the gay and rousing blade, was not encouraged. We
were very strictly 'gated,' though the whole society
once got out of window, and, by way of protest,
made a moonlight march into the country. We
attended ' gaudeamuses ' and *solatia*—University
suppers—but little ; indeed, he who writes does not
remember any such diversions of boys who beat the
floor, and break the glass. To plant the standard
of cricket in the remoter gardens of our country,
in a region devastated by golf, was our ambition,
and here we had no assistance at all from the
University. It was chiefly at lecture, at football
on the links, and in the debating societies that we
met our fellow-students ; like the celebrated starling,
'we could not get out,' except to permitted dinners
and evening parties. Consequently one could only
sketch student life with a hand faltering and un-

trained.   It was very different with Murray and his friends.   They were their own masters, could sit up to all hours, smoking, talking, and, I dare say, drinking.   As I gather from his letters, Murray drank nothing stronger than water.   There was a certain kind of humour in drink, he said, but he thought it was chiefly obvious to the sober spectator. As the sober spectator, he sang of violent delights which have. violent ends.   He may best be left to illustrate student life for himself.   The ' waster ' of whom he chants is the slang name borne by the local fast man.

THE WASTER SINGING AT
MIDNIGHT.

AFTER LONGFELLOW.

Loud he sang the song Ta Phershon
For his personal diversion,
Sang the chorus U-pi-dee,
Sang about the Barley Bree.

In that hour when all is quiet
Sang he songs of noise and riot,
In a voice so loud and queer
That I wakened up to hear.

Songs that distantly resembled
Those one hears from men assembled
In the old Cross Keys Hotel,
Only sung not half so well.

For the time of this ecstatic
Amateur was most erratic,
And he only hit the key
Once in every melody.

If "he wot prigs wot isn't his'n
Ven he's cotched is sent to prison,"
He who murders sleep might well
Adorn a solitary cell.

But, if no obliging peeler
Will arrest this midnight squealer,
My own peculiar arm of might
Must undertake the job to-night.

The following fragment is but doubtfully auto-biographical. 'The swift four-wheeler' seldom devastates the streets where, of old, the Archbishop's jackmen sliced Presbyterian professors with the claymore, as James Melville tells us :—

TO NUMBER 27X.

Beloved Peeler ! friend and guide
    And guard of many a midnight reeler,
None worthier, though the world is wide,
    Beloved Peeler.

Thou from before the swift four-wheeler
    Didst pluck me, and didst thrust aside
A strongly built provision-dealer

Who menaced me with blows, and cried
    'Come on ! come on !' O Paian, Healer,
Then but for thee I must have died,
    Beloved Peeler !

The following presentiment, though he was no 'waster,' may very well have been his own. He was only half Scotch, and not at all metaphysical :—

THE WASTER'S PRESENTIMENT

I shall be spun. There is a voice within
    Which tells me plainly I am all undone ;
For though I toil not, neither do I spin,
    I shall be spun.

April approaches.   I have not begun
   Schwegler or Mackintosh, nor will begin
Those lucid works till April 21.

So my degree I do not hope to win,
   For not by ways like mine degrees are won ;
And though, to please my uncle, I go in,
     I shall be spun.

Here we must quote, from *The Scarlet Gown*, one of his most tender pieces of affectionate praise bestowed on his favourite city :—

A DECEMBER DAY

Blue, blue is the sea to-day,
   Warmly the light
Sleeps on St. Andrews Bay—
   Blue, fringed with white.

That's no December sky !
   Surely 'tis June
Holds now her state on high,
   Queen of the noon.

Only the tree-tops bare
  Crowning the hill,
Clear-cut in perfect air,
  Warn us that still

Winter, the aged chief,
  Mighty in power,
Exiles the tender leaf,
  Exiles the flower.

Is there a heart to-day,
  A heart that grieves
For flowers that fade away,
  For fallen leaves?

Oh, not in leaves or flowers
  Endures the charm
That clothes those naked towers
  With love-light warm.

O dear St. Andrews Bay,
  Winter or Spring
Gives not nor takes away
  Memories that cling

All round thy girdling reefs,
  That walk thy shore,
Memories of joys and griefs
  Ours evermore.

'I have *not* worked for my classes this session,' he writes (1884), 'and shall not take any places.' The five or six most distinguished pupils used, at least in my time, to receive prize-books decorated with the University's arms. These prize-men, no doubt, held the 'places' alluded to by Murray. If *he* was idle, 'I speak of him but brotherly,' having never held any 'place' but that of second to Mr. Wallace, now Professor of Moral Philosophy at Oxford, in the Greek Class (Mr. Sellar's). Why was one so idle, in Latin (Mr. Shairp), in Morals (Mr. Ferrier), in Logic (Mr. Veitch)? but Logic was unintelligible.

'I must confess,' remarks Murray, in a similar spirit of pensive regret, 'that I have not had any ambition to distinguish myself either in Knight's (Moral Philosophy) or in Butler's.'[1]

Murray then speaks with some acrimony about earnest students, whose motive, he thinks, is a small ambition. But surely a man may be fond

[1] Mr. Butler lectures on Physics, or, as it is called in Scotland, Natural Philosophy.

of metaphysics for the sweet sake of Queen
Entelechy, and, moreover, these students looked
forward to days in which real work would bear
fruit.

'You must grind up the opinions of Plato,
Aristotle, and a lot of other men, concerning things
about which they knew nothing, and we know
nothing, taking these opinions at second or third
hand, and never looking into the works of these
men ; for to a man who wants to take a place,
there is no time for anything of that sort.'

Why not?   The philosophers ought to be read
in their own language, as they are now read.   The
remarks on the most fairy of philosophers—Plato ; on
the greatest of all minds, that of Aristotle, are boyish.
Again 'I speak but brotherly,' remembering an
old St. Leonard's essay in which Virgil was called
'the furtive Mantuan,' and another, devoted to
ridicule of Euripides.   But Plato and Aristotle we
never blasphemed.

Murray adds that he thinks, next year, of taking
the highest Greek Class, and English Literature.

In the latter, under Mr. Baynes, he took the first place, which he mentions casually to Mrs. Murray about a year after date :—

> 'A sweet life and an idle
>> He lives from year to year,
> Unknowing bit or bridle,
>> There are no Proctors here.'

In Greek, despite his enthusiastic admiration of the professor, Mr. Campbell, he did not much enjoy himself :—

> 'Thrice happy are those
>> Who ne'er heard of Greek Prose—
> Or Greek Poetry either, as far as that goes ;
>> For Liddell and Scott
>> Shall cumber them not,
> Nor Sargent nor Sidgwick shall break their repose.

> But I, late at night,
>> By the very bad light
> Of very bad gas, must painfully write
>> Some stuff that a Greek
>> With his delicate cheek
> Would smile at as 'barbarous'—faith, he well might.

So away with Greek Prose,
The source of my woes !
(This metre's too tough, I must draw to a close.)
May Sargent be drowned
In the ocean profound,
And Sidgwick be food for the carrion crows !'

Greek prose is a stubborn thing, and the biographer remembers being told that his was 'the
best, with the worst mistakes'; also frequently by
Mr. Sellar, that it was 'bald.' But Greek prose is
splendid practice, and no less good practice is
Greek and Latin verse. These exercises, so much
sneered at, are the Dwellers on the Threshold of
the life of letters. They are haunting forms of fear,
but they have to be wrestled with, like the Angel
(to change the figure), till they bless you, and make
words become, in your hands, like the clay of the
modeller. Could we write Greek like Mr. Jebb,
we would never write anything else.

Murray had naturally, it seems, certainly not by
dint of wrestling with Greek prose, the mastery of
language. His light verse is wonderfully handled,

d.

quaint, fluent, right. Modest as he was, he was
ambitious, as we said, but not ambitious of any
gain; merely eager, in his own way, to excel. His
ideal is plainly stated in the following verses:—

ΑΙΕΝ ΑΡΙΣΤΕΥΕΙΝ

Ever to be the best.   To lead
  In whatsoever things are true;
  Not stand among the halting crew,
The faint of heart, the feeble-kneed,
Who tarry for a certain sign
  To make them follow with the rest—
Oh, let not their reproach be thine!
  But ever be the best.

For want of this aspiring soul,
  Great deeds on earth remain undone,
  But, sharpened by the sight of one,
Many shall press toward the goal.
Thou running foremost of the throng,
  The fire of striving in thy breast,
Shalt win, although the race be long,
  And ever be the best.

And wilt thou question of the prize?
  'Tis not of silver or of gold,
  Nor in applauses manifold,
But hidden in the heart it lies:

To know that but for thee not one
　　Had run the race or sought the quest,
To know that thou hast ever done
　　And ever been the best.

Murray was never a great athlete : his ambition
did not lead him to desire a place in the Scottish
Fifteen at Football.　Probably he was more likely
to be found matched against ' The Man from Inversnaid.'

IMITATED FROM WORDSWORTH

He brought a team from Inversnaid
　　To play our Third Fifteen,
A man whom none of us had played
　　And very few had seen.

He weighed not less than eighteen stone,
　　And to a practised eye
He seemed as little fit to run
　　As he was fit to fly.

He looked so clumsy and so slow,
　　And made so little fuss ;
But he got in behind—and oh,
　　The difference to us !

He was never a golfer; one of his best light pieces, published later in the *Saturday Review*, dealt in kindly ridicule of *The City of Golf*.

> 'Would you like to see a city given over,
>   Soul and body, to a tyrannising game?
> If you would, there's little need to be a rover,
>   For St. Andrews is the abject city's name.'

He was fond, too fond, of long midnight walks, for in these he overtasked his strength, and he had all a young man's contempt for maxims about not sitting in wet clothes and wet boots. Early in his letters he speaks of bad colds, and it is matter of tradition that he despised flannel. Most of us have been like him, and have found pleasure in wading Tweed, for example, when chill with snaw-bree. In brief, while reading about Murray's youth most men must feel that they are reading, with slight differences, about their own. He writes thus of his long darkling tramps, in a rhymed epistle to his friend C. C. C.

> 'And I fear we never again shall go,
>   The cold and weariness scorning,
> For a ten mile walk through the frozen snow
>   At one o'clock in the morning:

Out by Cameron, in by the Grange,
  And to bed as the moon descended . . .
To you and to me there has come a change,
  And the days of our youth are ended.'

One fancies him roaming solitary, after midnight,
in the dark deserted streets. He passes the deep
porch of the College Church, and the spot where
Patrick Hamilton was burned. He goes down to
the Castle by the sea, where, some say, the murdered
Cardinal may now and again be seen, in his red hat.
In South Street he hears the roll and rattle of the
viewless carriage which sounds in that thoroughfare.
He loiters under the haunted tower on Hepburn's
precinct wall, the tower where the lady of the bright
locks lies, with white gloves on her hands. Might
he not share, in the desolate Cathedral, *La Messe des
Morts*, when all the lost souls of true lovers are
allowed to meet once a year. Here be they who
were too fond when Culdees ruled, or who loved
young monks of the Priory ; here be ladies of Queen
Mary's Court, and the fair inscrutable Queen her-
self, with Chastelard, that died at St. Andrews for

desire of her; and poor lassies and lads who were over gay for Andrew Melville and Mr. Blair; and Miss Pett, who tended young Montrose, and may have had a tenderness for his love-locks. They are a *triste* good company, tender and true, as the lovers of whom M. Anatole France has written (*La Messe des Morts*). Above the witches' lake come shadows of the women who suffered under Knox and the Bastard of Scotland, poor creatures burned to ashes with none to help or pity. The shades of Dominicans flit by the Black Friars wall—verily the place is haunted, and among Murray's pleasures was this of pacing alone, by night, in that airy press and throng of those who lived and loved and suffered so long ago—

· 'The mist hangs round the College tower,
    The ghostly street
Is silent at this midnight hour,
    Save for my feet.

With none to see, with none to hear,
    Downward I go
To where, beside the rugged pier,
    The sea sings low.

It sings a tune well loved and known
        In days gone by,
When often here, and not alone,
        I watched the sky.'

But he was not always, nor often, lonely. He was fond of making his speech at the Debating Societies, and his speeches are remembered as good. If he declined the whisky and water, he did not flee the weed. I borrow from *College Echoes*—

A TENNYSONIAN FRAGMENT

So in the village inn the poet dwelt.
His honey-dew was gone ; only the pouch,
His cousin's work, her empty labour, left.
But still he sniffed it, still a fragrance clung
And lingered all about the broidered flowers.
Then came his landlord, saying in broad Scotch,
' Smoke plug, mon,' whom he looked at doubtfully.
Then came the grocer saying, ' Hae some twist
At tippence,' whom he answered with a qualm.
But when they left him to himself again,
Twist, like a fiend's breath from a distant room
Diffusing through the passage, crept ; the smell
Deepening had power upon him, and he mixt
His fancies with the billow-lifted bay
Of Biscay, and the rollings of a ship.

And on that night he made a little song,
And called his song 'The Song of Twist and Plug,'
And sang it ; scarcely could he make or sing.

'Rank is black plug, though smoked in wind and rain ;
And rank is twist, which gives no end of pain ;
I know not which is ranker, no, not I.

'Plug, art thou rank? then milder twist must be ;
Plug, thou art milder : rank is twist to me.
O twist, if plug be milder, let me buy.

'Rank twist, that seems to make me fade away,
Rank plug, that navvies smoke in loveless clay,
I know not which is ranker, no, not I.

'I fain would purchase flake, if that could be ;
I needs must purchase plug, ah, woe is me !
Plug and a cutty, a cutty, let me buy.

His was the best good thing of the night's talk, and
the thing that was remembered. He excited himself
a good deal over Rectorial Elections. The duties of
the Lord Rector and the mode of his election have
varied frequently in near five hundred years. In
Murray's day, as in my own, the students elected their

own Rector, and before Lord Bute's energetic reign,
the Rector had little to do, but to make a speech,
and give a prize.   I vaguely remember proposing the
author of *Tom Brown* long ago : he was not, however, in the running.

Politics often inspire the electors; occasionally
(I have heard) grave seniors use their influence,
mainly for reasons of academic policy.

In December 1887 Murray writes about an
election in which Mr. Lowell was a candidate.   ' A
pitiful protest was entered by an ' (epithets followed
by a proper name) 'against Lowell, on the score of
his being an alien.   Mallock, as you learn, was
withdrawn, for which I am truly thankful.'   Unlucky
Mr. Mallock !   ' Lowell polled 100 and Gibson 92.
. . . The intrigues and corruption appear to be
almost worthy of an American Presidential election.'
Mr. Lowell could not accept a compliment which
pleased him, because of his official position, and the
misfortune of his birth !

Murray was already doing a very little ' miniature
journalism,' in the form of University Notes for a

local paper. He complains of the ultra Caledonian frankness with which men told him that they were very bad. A needless, if friendly, outspokenness was a feature in Scottish character which he did not easily endure. He wrote a good deal of verse in the little University paper, now called *College Echoes*.

If Murray ever had any definite idea of being ordained for the ministry in any 'denomination,' he abandoned it. His 'bursaries' (scholarships or exhibitions), on which he had been passing rich, expired, and he had to earn a livelihood. It seems plain to myself that he might easily have done so with his pen. A young friend of my own (who will excuse me for thinking that his bright verses are not *better* than Murray's) promptly made, by these alone, an income which to Murray would have been affluence. But this could not be done at St. Andrews. Again, Murray was not in contact with people in the centre of newspapers and magazines. He went very little into general society, even at St. Andrews, and thus failed, perhaps, to make acquaintances who might have been 'useful.' He would have scorned the idea of making useful acquaintances. But without seeking them, why should we reject any friendliness when it offers itself? We are all members one of another. Murray speaks of his experience of human beings, as rich in examples of kindness and good-will. His shyness, his reserve, his extreme unselfishness,—carried to the point of diffidence,—made him rather shun than seek older people who were dangerously likely to be serviceable. His manner, when once he could be induced to meet strangers, was extremely frank and pleasant, but from meeting strangers he shrunk, in his inveterate modesty.

In 1886 Murray had the misfortune to lose his father, and it became, perhaps, more prominently needful that he should find a profession. He now assisted Professor Meiklejohn of St. Andrews in various kinds of literary and academic work, and in him found a friend, with whom he remained in close intercourse to the last. He began the weary path, which all literary beginners must tread, of sending contributions to magazines. He seldom read magazine articles. 'I do not greatly care for

" problems " and " vexed questions."   I am so much
of a problem and a vexed question that I have
quite enough to do in searching for a solution of
my own personality.'   He tried a story, based on
'a midnight experience' of his own ; unluckily he
does not tell us what that experience was.   Had
he encountered one of the local ghosts ?

   ' My blood-curdling romance I offered to the
editor of *Longman's Magazine*, but that misguided
person was so ill-advised as to return it, accompanied with one of these abominable lithographed
forms conveying his hypocritical regrets.'   Murray
sent a directed envelope with a twopenny-halfpenny
stamp.   The paper came back for three-halfpence
by book-post.   ' I have serious thoughts of sueing
him for the odd penny !'   'Why should people be
fools enough to read my rot when they have twenty
volumes of Scott at their command?'   He con-
fesses to 'a Scott-mania almost as intense as if he
were the last new sensation.'   'I was always fond
of him, but I am fonder than ever now.'   This
plunge into the immortal romances seems really to

have discouraged Murray; at all events he says very little more about attempts in fiction of his own. 'I am a barren rascal,' he writes, quoting Johnson on Fielding. Like other men, Murray felt extreme difficulty in writing articles or tales which have an infinitesimal chance of being accepted. It needs a stout heart to face this almost fixed certainty of rejection: a man is weakened by his apprehensions of a lithographed form, and of his old manuscript coming home to roost, like the Graces of Theocritus, to pine in the dusty chest where is their chill abode. If the Alexandrian poets knew this ill-fortune, so do all beginners in letters. There is nothing for it but 'putting a stout heart to a stey brae,' as the Scotch proverb says. Editors want good work, and on finding a new man who is good, they greatly rejoice. But it is so difficult to do vigorous and spontaneous work, as it were, in the dark. Murray had not, it is probable, the qualities of the novelist, the narrator. An excellent critic he might have been if he had 'descended to criticism,' but he had, at this time, no introductions, and probably

did not address reviews at random to editors. As
to poetry, these much-vexed men receive such
enormous quantities of poetry that they usually
reject it at a venture, and obtain the small necessary
supplies from agreeable young ladies. Had Murray
been in London, with a few literary friends, he
might soon have been a thriving writer of light
prose and light verse. But the enchantress held
him ; he hated London, he had no literary friends,
he could write gaily for pleasure, not for gain. So,
like the Scholar Gypsy, he remained contemplative,

' Waiting for the spark from heaven to fall.'

About this time the present writer was in St.
Andrews as Gifford Lecturer in Natural Theology.
To say that an enthusiasm for totems and taboos,
ghosts and gods of savage men, was aroused by
these lectures, would be to exaggerate unpardon-
ably. Efforts to make the students write essays
or ask questions were so entire a failure that only
one question was received—as to the proper pro-
nunciation of ' Myth.' Had one been fortunate

enough to interest Murray, it must have led to some discussion of his literary attempts. He mentions having attended a lecture given by myself to the Literary Society on ' Literature as a Profession,' and he found the lecturer ' far more at home in such a subject than in the Gifford Lectures.' Possibly the hearer was 'more at home' in literature than in discussions as to the origin of Huitzilopochtli. ' Literature,' he says, 'never was, is not, and never will be, in the ordinary sense of the term, a profession. You can't teach it as you can the professions, you can't succeed in it as you can in the professions, by dint of mere diligence and without special aptitude. . . . I think all this chatter about the technical and pecuniary sides of literature is extremely foolish and worse than useless. It only serves to glut the idle curiosity of the general public about matters with which they have no concern, a curiosity which (thanks partly to American methods of journalism) has become simply outrageous.'

Into chatter about the pecuniary aspect of literature the Lecturer need hardly say that he did not

meander. It is absolutely true that literature cannot be taught. Maupassant could have dispensed
with the instructions of Flaubert. But an 'aptitude'
is needed in all professions, and in such arts as
music, and painting, and sculpture, teaching is
necessary. In literature, teaching can only come
from general education in letters, from experience,
from friendly private criticism. But if you cannot
succeed in literature 'by dint of mere diligence,'
mere diligence is absolutely essential. Men must
read, must observe, must practise. Diligence is as
necessary to the author as to the grocer, the solicitor,
the dentist, the barrister, the soldier. Nothing but
nature can give the aptitude ; diligence must improve
it, and experience may direct it. It is not enough
to wait for the spark from heaven to fall ; the spark
must be caught, and tended, and cherished. A man
must labour till he finds his vein, and himself.
Again, if literature is an art, it is also a profession.
A man's very first duty is to support himself and
those, if any, who are dependent on him. If he
cannot do it by epics, tragedies, lyrics, he must do

it by articles, essays, tales, or how he honestly can. He must win his leisure by his labour, and give his leisure to his art. Murray, at this time, was diligent in helping to compile and correct educational works. He might, but for the various conditions of reserve, hatred of towns, and the rest, have been earning his leisure by work more brilliant and more congenial to most men. But his theory of literature was so lofty that he probably found the other, the harder, the less remunerative, the less attractive work, more congenial to his tastes.

He describes, to Mrs. Murray, various notable visitors to St. Andrews: Professor Butcher, who lectured on Lucian, and is 'very handsome,' Mr. Arthur Balfour, the Lord Rector, who is 'rather handsome,' and delights the listener by his eloquence; Mr. Chamberlain, who pleases him too, though he finds Mr. Chamberlain rather acrimonious in his political reflections. About Lucian, the subject of Mr. Butcher's lecture, Murray says nothing. That brilliant man of letters in general, the Alcibiades of literature, the wittiest, and, rarely, the

e

most tender, and, always, the most graceful, was a
model who does not seem to have attracted Murray.
Lucian amused, and amuses, and lived by amusing :
the vein of romance and poetry that was his he
worked but rarely : perhaps the Samosatene did not
take himself too seriously, yet he lives through the
ages, an example, in many ways to be followed, of a
man who obviously delighted in all that he wrought.
He was no model to Murray, who only delighted in
his moments of inspiration, and could not make
himself happy even in the trifles which are demanded
from the professional pen.

He did, at last, endeavour to ply that servile
engine of which Pendennis conceived so exalted an
opinion. Certainly a false pride did not stand in
his way when, on May 5, 1889, he announced that
he was about to leave St. Andrews, and attempt to
get work at proof-correcting and in the humblest
sorts of journalism in Edinburgh. The chapter is
honourable to his resolution, but most melancholy.
There were competence and ease waiting for him,
probably, in London, if he would but let his pen

have its way in bright comment and occasional verse. But he chose the other course. With letters of introduction from Mr. Meiklejohn, he consulted the houses of Messrs. Clark and Messrs. Constable in Edinburgh. He did not find that his knowledge of Greek was adequate to the higher and more remunerative branches of proof-reading, that weary meticulous toil, so fatiguing to the eyesight. The hours, too, were very long; he could do more and better work in fewer hours. No time, no strength, were left for reading and writing. He did, while in Edinburgh, send a few things to magazines, but he did not actually 'bombard' editors. He is 'to live in one room, and dine, if not on a red herring, on the next cheapest article of diet.' These months of privation, at which he laughed, and some weeks of reading proofs, appear to have quite undermined health which was never strong, and which had been sorely tried by 'the wind of a cursed to-day, the curse of a windy to-morrow,' at St. Andrews. If a reader observes in Murray a lack of strenuous diligence, he must attribute it less to lack of resolu-

tion, than to defect of physical force and energy.
The many bad colds of which he speaks were
warnings of the end, which came in the form of
consumption. This lurking malady it was that made
him wait, and dally with his talent. He hit on the
idea of translating some of Bossuet's orations for a
Scotch theological publisher. Alas! the publisher
did not anticipate a demand, among Scotch ministers,
for the Eagle of Meaux. Murray, in his innocence,
was startled by the caution of the publisher, who
certainly would have been a heavy loser. 'I
honestly believe that, if Charles Dickens were now
alive and unknown, and were to offer the MS. of *Pickwick* to an Edinburgh publisher, that sagacious old in-
dividual would shake his prudent old head, and refuse
(with the utmost politeness) to publish it!' There
is a good deal of difference between *Pickwick* and a
translation of old French sermons about Madame,
and Condé, and people of whom few modern readers
ever heard.

Alone, in Edinburgh, Murray was saddened by
the 'unregarding' irresponsive faces of the people

as they passed. In St. Andrews he probably knew
every face; even in Edinburgh (a visitor from
London thinks) there is a friendly look among the
passers. Murray did not find it so. He approached
a newspaper office: 'he [the Editor whom he met]
was extremely frank, and told me that the tone of my
article on ———— was underbred, while the verses I
had sent him had nothing in them. Very pleasant
for the feelings of a young author, was it not? . . .
Unfavourable criticism is an excellent tonic, but it
should be a little diluted. . . . I must, however, do
him the justice to say that he did me a good turn by
introducing me to ————, . . . who was kind and
encouraging in the extreme.'

Murray now called on the Editor of the *Scottish
Leader*, the Gladstonian organ, whom he found very
courteous. He was asked to write some 'leader-
notes' as they are called, paragraphs which appear
in the same columns as the leading articles. These
were published, to his astonishment, and he was 'to
be taken on at a salary of ———— a week.' Let us
avoid pecuniary chatter, and merely say that the

sum, while he was on trial, was not likely to tempt
many young men into the career of journalism.
Yet 'the work will be very exacting, and almost
preclude the possibility of my doing anything else.'
Now, as four leader notes, or, say, six, can be written
in an hour, it is difficult to see the necessity for this
fatigue. Probably there were many duties more exacting, and less agreeable, than the turning out of
epigrams. Indeed there was other work of some
more or less mechanical kind, and the manufacture
of 'leader notes' was the least part of Murray's
industry. At the end of two years there was 'the
prospect of a very fair salary.' But there was 'night-
work and everlasting hurry.' 'The interviewing of
a half-bred Town-Councillor on the subject of gas
and paving' did not exhilarate Murray. Again, he
had to compile a column of Literary News, from the
Athenæum, the *Academy*, and so on, 'with comments
and enlargements where possible.' This might have
been made extremely amusing, it sounds like a
delightful task,—the making of comments on ' Mr.
—— has finished a sonnet :' ' Mr. ——'s poems are

in their fiftieth thousand:' 'Miss —— has gone on
a tour of health to the banks of the Yang-tse-kiang:'
'Mrs. —— is engaged on a novel about the Pilchard
Fishery.' One could make comments (if permitted)
on these topics for love, and they might not be
unpopular. But perhaps Murray was shackled a
little by human respect, or the prejudices of his
editor. At all events he calls it 'not very inspiring
employment.' The bare idea, I confess, inspirits
me extremely.

But the literary *follet*, who delights in mild
mischief, did not haunt Murray. He found an
opportunity to write on the Canongate Churchyard,
where Fergusson lies, under the monument erected
by Burns to the boy of genius whom he called his
master. Of course the part of the article which
dealt with Fergusson, himself a poet of the Scarlet
Gown, was cut out. The Scotch do not care to
hear about Fergusson, in spite of their 'myriad
mutchkined enthusiasm' for his more illustrious
imitator and successor, Burns.

At this time Edinburgh was honouring itself, and

Mr. Parnell, by conferring its citizenship on that patriot. Murray was actually told off 'to stand at a given point of the line on which the hero marched, and to write some lines of 'picturesque description.' This kind of thing could not go on. It was at Nelson's Monument that he stood : his enthusiasm was more for Nelson than for Mr. Parnell; and he caught a severe cold on this noble occasion. Murray's opinions clashed with those of the *Scottish Leader*, and he withdrew from its service.

Just a week passed between the Parnellian triumph and Murray's retreat from daily journalism. 'On a newspaper one must have no opinions except those which are favourable to the sale of the paper and the filling of its advertisement columns.' That is not precisely an accurate theory. Without knowing anything of the circumstances, one may imagine that Murray was rather impracticable. Of course he could not write against his own opinions, but it is unusual to expect any one to do that, or to find any one who will do it. 'Incompatibility of temper' probably caused this secession from the newspaper.

After various attempts to find occupation, he did some proof-reading for Messrs. Constable. Among other things he 'read' the Journal of Lady Mary Coke, privately printed for Lord Home. Lady Mary, who appears as a lively child in *The Heart of Midlothian*, 'had a taste for loo, gossip, and gardening, but the greatest of these is gossip.' The best part of the book is Lady Louisa Stuart's inimitable introduction. Early in October he decided to give up proof-reading: the confinement had already told on his health. In the letter which announces this determination he describes a sermon of Principal Caird: 'Voice, gesture, language, thought—all in the highest degree,—combined to make it the most moving and exalted speech of a man to men that I ever listened to.' 'The world is too much with me,' he adds, as if he and the world were ever friends, or ever likely to be friendly.

October 27th found him dating from St. Andrews

again. 'St. Andrews after Edinburgh is Paradise.'
His Dalilah had called him home to her, and he
was never again unfaithful. He worked for his
firm friend, Professor Meiklejohn, he undertook
some teaching, and he wrote a little. It was at this
time that his biographer made Murray's acquaintance.
I had been delighted with his verses in *College
Echoes*, and I asked him to bring me some of his
more serious work. But he never brought them:
his old enemy, reserve, overcame him. A few of
his pieces were published 'At the Sign of the Ship'
in *Longman's Magazine*, to which he contributed
occasionally.

From this point there is little in Murray's life to
be chronicled. In 1890 his health broke down
entirely, and consumption declared itself. Very
early in 1891 he visited Egypt, where it was thought
that some educational work might be found for
him. But he found Egypt cold, wet, and windy; of
Alexandria and the Mediterranean he says little:
indeed he was almost too weak and ill to see
what is delightful either in nature or art.

'To aching eyes each landscape lowers,
   To feverish pulse each gale blows chill,
And Araby's or Eden's bowers
   Were barren as this moorland hill,'

says the least self-conscious of poets. Even so
barren were the rich Nile and so bleak the blue
Mediterranean waters. Though received by the
kindest and most hospitable friends, Murray was
homesick, and pined to be in England, now that
spring was there. He made the great mistake
of coming home too early. At Ilminster, in his
mother's home, he slowly faded out of life. I have
not the heart to quote his descriptions of brief yet
laborious saunters in the coppices, from the letters
which he wrote to the lady of his heart. He was
calm, cheerful, even buoyant. His letters to his
college friends are all concerned with literature, or
with happy old times, and are full of interest in
them and in their happiness.

He was not wholly idle. He wrote a number of
short pieces of verse in *Punch*, and two or three in
the *St. James's Gazette*. Other work, no doubt, he

planned, but his strength was gone. In 1891 his book, *The Scarlet Gown*, was published by his friend, Mr. A. M. Holden. The little volume, despite its local character, was kindly received by the Reviews. Here, it was plain, we had a poet who was to St. Andrews what the regretted J. K. S. was to Eton and Cambridge. This measure of success was not calculated to displease our *alumnus addictissimus*.

Friendship and love, he said, made the summer of 1892 very happy to him. I last heard from him in the summer of 1893, when he sent me some of his most pleasing verses. He was in Scotland; he had wandered back, a shadow of himself, to his dear St. Andrews. I conceived that he was better; he said nothing about his health. It is not easy to quote from his letters to his friend, Mr. Wallace, still written in his beautiful firm hand. They are too full of affectionate banter: they also contain criticisms on living poets: he shows an admiration, discriminating and not wholesale, of Mr. Kipling's verse: he censures Mr. Swinburne, whose Jacobite song (as he wrote to myself) did not precisely strike him as the kind of thing that Jacobites used to sing.

They certainly celebrated

> 'The faith our fathers fought for,
> The kings our fathers knew,'

in a different tone in the North.

The perfect health of mind, in these letters of a dying man, is admirable. Reading old letters over, he writes to Miss ——, 'I have known a wonderful number of wonderfully kind-hearted people.' That is his criticism of a world which had given him but a scanty welcome, and a life of foiled endeavour, of disappointed hope. Even now there was a disappointment. His poems did not find a publisher: what publisher can take the risk of adding another volume of poetry to the enormous stock of verse brought out at the author's expense? This did not sour or sadden him: he took Montaigne's advice, 'not to make too much marvel of our own fortunes.'

His biographer, hearing in the winter of 1893 that Murray's illness was now considered hopeless, though its rapid close was not expected, began, with Professor Meiklejohn, to make arrangements for the publication of the poems. But the poet did not live to have this poor gratification. He died in the early hours of 1894.

Of the merits of his more serious poetry others must speak. To the Editor it seems that he is always at his best when he is inspired by the Northern Sea, and the long sands and grey sea grasses. Then he is most himself. He was improving in his art with every year: his development, indeed, was somewhat late.

It is less of the writer than the man that we prefer to think. His letters display, in passages which he would not have desired to see quoted, the depth and tenderness and thoughtfulness of his affections. He must have been a delightful friend: illness could not make him peevish, and his correspondence with old college companions could never be taken for that of a consciously dying man. He had perfect courage, and resolution even in his seeming irresoluteness. He was resolved to be, and continued to be, himself

'He had kept the bird in his bosom.' We, who regret him, may wish that he had been granted a longer life, and a secure success. Happier fortunes might have mellowed him, no fortunes could have altered for the worse his admirable nature. He lives in the hearts of his friends, and in the pride and sympathy of those who, after him, have worn and shall wear the scarlet gown.

The following examples of his poetry were selected by Murray's biographer from a considerable mass, and have been seen through the press by Professor Meiklejohn, who possesses the original manuscript, beautifully written.

Far from that bleak and rude land
   An exile I remain
Fixed in a fair and good land,
   A valley and a plain
Rich in fat fields and woodland,
   And watered well with rain.

Last night the full moon's splendour
   Shone down on Taunton Dene,
And pasture fresh and tender,
   And coppice dusky green,
The heavenly light did render
   In one enchanted scene,

One fair unearthly vision.
   Yet soon mine eyes were cloyed,
And found those fields Elysian
   Too rich to be enjoyed.
Or was it our division
   Made all my pleasure void?

Across the window glasses
> The curtain then I drew,
And, as a sea-bird passes,
> In sleep my spirit flew
To grey and windswept grasses
> And moonlit sands—and you.

WINTER AT ST. ANDREWS

THE city once again doth wear
    Her wonted dress of winter's bride,
Her mantle woven of misty air,
    With saffron sunlight faintly dyed.
She sits above the seething tide,
    Of all her summer robes forlorn—
And dead is all her summer pride—
    The leaves are off Queen Mary's Thorn.

All round, the landscape stretches bare,
    The bleak fields lying far and wide,
Monotonous, with here and there
    A lone tree on a lone hillside.

4

No more the land is glorified
  With golden gleams of ripening corn,
Scarce is a cheerful hue descried—
  The leaves are off Queen Mary's Thorn.

For me, I do not greatly care
  Though leaves be dead, and mists abide.
To me the place is thrice as fair
  In winter as in summer-tide:
With kindlier memories allied
  Of pleasure past and pain o'erworn.
What care I, though the earth may hide
  The leaves from off Queen Mary's Thorn?

Thus I unto my friend replied,
  When, on a chill late autumn morn,
He pointed to the tree, and cried,
  'The leaves are off Queen Mary's Thorn!'

PATRIOTISM

THERE was a time when it was counted high
To be a patriot—whether by the zeal
Of peaceful labour for the country's weal,
Or by the courage in her cause to die:

For King and Country was a rallying cry
That turned men's hearts to fire, their nerves to
steel;
Not to unheeding ears did it appeal,
A pulpit formula, a platform lie.

Only a fool will wantonly desire
That war should come, outpouring blood and fire,
And bringing grief and hunger in her train.
And yet, if there be found no other way,
God send us war, and with it send the day
When love of country shall be real again!

6

SLEEP FLIES ME

SLEEP flies me like a lover
  Too eagerly pursued,
Or like a bird to cover
  Within some distant wood,
Where thickest boughs roof over
  Her secret solitude.

The nets I spread to snare her,
  Although with cunning wrought,
Have only served to scare her,
  And now she 'll not be caught.
To those who best could spare her,
  She ever comes unsought.

7

She lights upon their pillows ;
　She gives them pleasant dreams,
Grey-green with leaves of willows,
　And cool with sound of streams,
Or big with tranquil billows,
　On which the starlight gleams.

No vision fair entrances
　My weary open eye,
No marvellous romances
　Make night go swiftly by ;
But only feverish fancies
　Beset me where I lie.

The black midnight is steeping
　The hillside and the lawn,
But still I lie unsleeping,
　With curtains backward drawn,
To catch the earliest peeping
　Of the desirèd dawn.

Perhaps, when day is breaking ;

When birds their song begin,

And, worn with all night waking,

I call their music din,

Sweet sleep, some pity taking,

At last may enter in.

LOVE'S PHANTOM

Whene'er I try to read a book,
Across the page your face will look,
And then I neither know nor care
What sense the printed words may bear.

At night when I would go to sleep,
Thinking of you, awake I keep,
And still repeat the words you said,
Like sick men murmuring prayers in bed.

And when, with weariness oppressed,
I sink in spite of you to rest,
Your image, like a lovely sprite,
Haunts me in dreams through half the night.

10

I wake upon the autumn morn
To find the sunrise hardly born,
And in the sky a soft pale blue,
And in my heart your image true.

When out I walk to take the air,
Your image is for ever there,
Among the woods that lose their leaves,
Or where the North Sea sadly heaves.

By what enchantment shall be laid
This ghost, which does not make afraid,
But vexes with dim loveliness
And many a shadowy caress?

There is no other way I know
But unto you forthwith to go,
That I may look upon the maid
Whereof that other is the shade.

As the strong sun puts out the moon,

Whose borrowed rays are all his own,

So, in your living presence, dies

The phantom kindled at your eyes.

By this most blessed spell, each day

The vexing ghost awhile I lay.

Yet am I glad to know that when

I leave you it will rise again.

COME BACK TO ST. ANDREWS

Come back to St. Andrews! Before you went away
You said you would be wretched where you could
not see the Bay,
The East sands and the West sands and the castle
in the sea
Come back to St. Andrews—St. Andrews and me.

Oh, it's dreary along South Street when the rain is
coming down,
And the east wind makes the student draw more
close his warm red gown,
As I often saw you do, when I watched you going by
On the stormy days to College, from my window up
on high.

13

I wander on the Lade Braes, where I used to walk
with you,

And purple are the woods of Mount Melville,
budding new,

But I cannot bear to look, for the tears keep
coming so,

And the Spring has lost the freshness which it had
a year ago.

Yet often I could fancy, where the pathway takes a
turn,

I shall see you in a moment, coming round beside
the burn,

Coming round beside the burn, with your swinging
step and free,

And your face lit up with pleasure at the sudden
sight of me.

Beyond the Rock and Spindle, where we watched
the water clear

In the happy April sunshine, with a happy sound
to hear,

There I sat this afternoon, but no hand was holding
mine,

And the water sounded eerie, though the April sun
did shine.

Oh, why should I complain of what I know was
bound to be?

For you had your way to make, and you must not
think of me.

But a woman's heart is weak, and a woman's joys
are few—

There are times when I could die for a moment's
sight of you.

It may be you will come again, before my hair is
   grey
As the sea is in the twilight of a weary winter's day.
When success is grown a burden, and your heart
   would fain be free,
Come back to St. Andrews—St. Andrews and me.

THE SOLITARY

I HAVE been lonely all my days on earth,
    Living a life within my secret soul,
With mine own springs of sorrow and of mirth,
    Beyond the world's control.

Though sometimes with vain longing I have sought
    To walk the paths where other mortals tread,
To wear the clothes for other mortals wrought,
    And eat the selfsame bread—

Yet have I ever found, when thus I strove
    To mould my life upon the common plan,
That I was furthest from all truth and love,
    And least a living man.

Truth frowned upon my poor hypocrisy,

　　Life left my soul, and dwelt but in my sense ;

No man could love me, for all men could see

　　The hollow vain pretence.

Their clothes sat on me with outlandish air,

　　Upon their easy road I tripped and fell,

And still I sickened of the wholesome fare

　　On which they nourished well.

I was a stranger in that company,

　　A Galilean whom his speech bewrayed,

And when they lifted up their songs of glee,

　　My voice sad discord made.

Peace for mine own self I could never find,

　　And still my presence marred the general peace,

And when I parted, leaving them behind,

　　They felt, and I, release.

So will I follow now my spirit's bent,
   Not scorning those who walk the beaten track,
Yet not despising mine own banishment,
    Nor often looking back.

Their way is best for them, but mine for me.
   And there is comfort for my lonely heart,
To think perhaps our journeys' ends may be
    Not very far apart.

TO ALFRED TENNYSON

1883

FAMILIAR with thy melody,
  We go debating of its power,
  As churls, who hear it hour by hour,
Contemn the skylark's minstrelsy—

As shepherds on a Highland lea
  Think lightly of the heather flower
  Which makes the moorland's purple dower,
As far away as eye can see.

Let churl or shepherd change his sky,
  And labour in the city dark,
    Where there is neither air nor room—
How often will the exile sigh
  To hear again the unwearied lark,
    And see the heather's lavish bloom !

ICHABOD

GONE is the glory from the hills,
    The autumn sunshine from the mere,
    Which mourns for the declining year
In all her tributary rills.

A sense of change obscurely chills
    The misty twilight atmosphere,
    In which familiar things appear
Like alien ghosts, foreboding ills.

The twilight hour a month ago
    Was full of pleasant warmth and ease,
    The pearl of all the twenty-four.
Erelong the winter gales shall blow,
    Erelong the winter frosts shall freeze—
    And oh, that it were June once more!

AT A HIGH CEREMONY

Not the proudest damsel here
Looks so well as doth my dear.
All the borrowed light of dress
Outshining not her loveliness,

A loveliness not born of art,
But growing outwards from her heart,
Illuminating all her face,
And filling all her form with grace.

Said I, of dress the borrowed light
Could rival not her beauty bright?
Yet, looking round, 'tis truth to tell,
No damsel here is dressed so well.

Only in them the dress one sees,
Because more greatly it doth please
Than any other charm that 's theirs,
Than all their manners, all their airs.

But dress in her, although indeed
It perfect be, we do not heed,
Because the face, the form, the air
Are all so gentle and so rare.

THE WASTED DAY

ANOTHER day let slip ! Its hours have run,
Its golden hours, with prodigal excess,
All run to waste. A day of life the less ;
Of many wasted days, alas, but one !

Through my west window streams the setting sun.
I kneel within my chamber, and confess
My sin and sorrow, filled with vain distress,
In place of honest joy for work well done.

At noon I passed some labourers in a field.
The sweat ran down upon each sunburnt face,
Which shone like copper in the ardent glow.
And one looked up, with envy unconcealed,
Beholding my cool cheeks and listless pace,
Yet he was happier, though he did not know.

24

INDOLENCE

FAIN would I shake thee off, but weak am I
   Thy strong solicitations to withstand.
   Plenty of work lies ready to my hand,
Which rests irresolute, and lets it lie.

How can I work, when that seductive sky
   Smiles through the window, beautiful and bland,
   And seems to half entreat and half command
My presence out of doors beneath its eye?

Will not the air be fresh, the water blue,
   The smell of beanfields, blowing to the shore,
      Better than these poor drooping purchased
        flowers?
Good-bye, dull books! Hot room, good-bye to you!
   And think it strange if I return before
      The sea grows purple in the evening hours.

DAWN SONG

I HEAR a twittering of birds,
   And now they burst in song.
How sweet, although it wants the words!
   It shall not want them long,
For I will set some to the note
Which bubbles from the thrush's throat.

O jewelled night, that reign'st on high,
   Where is thy crescent moon?
Thy stars have faded from the sky,
   The sun is coming soon.
The summer night is passed away,
Sing welcome to the summer day.

CAIRNSMILL DEN

TUNE: 'A ROVING'

As I, with hopeless love o'erthrown,
With love o'erthrown, with love o'erthrown,
 And this is truth I tell,
As I, with hopeless love o'erthrown,
Was sadly walking all alone,

  I met my love one morning
   In Cairnsmill Den.
  One morning, one morning,
  One blue and blowy morning,
  I met my love one morning
   In Cairnsmill Den.

A dead bough broke within the wood
Within the wood, within the wood,
 And this is truth I tell.
A dead bough broke within the wood,
And I looked up, and there she stood.

I asked what was it brought her there,
What brought her there, what brought her there,
 And this is truth I tell.
I asked what was it brought her there.
Says she, 'To pull the primrose fair.'

Says I, 'Come, let me pull with you,
Along with you, along with you,'
 And this is truth I tell.
Says I, 'Come let me pull with you,
For one is not so good as two.'

But when at noon we climbed the hill,

We climbed the hill, we climbed the hill,

   And this is truth I tell.

But when at noon we climbed the hill,

Her hands and mine were empty still.

And when we reached the top so high,

The top so high, the top so high,

   And this is truth I tell.

And when we reached the top so high

Says I, ' I 'll kiss you, if I die ! '

I kissed my love in Cairnsmill Den,

In Cairnsmill Den, in Cairnsmill Den,

   And this is truth I tell.

I kissed my love in Cairnsmill Den,

And my love kissed me back again.

I met my love one morning
    In Cairnsmill Den.
One morning, one morning,
One blue and blowy morning,
I met my love one morning
    In Cairnsmill Den.

A LOST OPPORTUNITY

ONE dark, dark night—it was long ago,
  The air was heavy and still and warm—
It fell to me and a man I know,
  To see two girls to their father's farm.

There was little seeing, that I recall :
  We seemed to grope in a cave profound.
They might have come by a painful fall,
  Had we not helped them over the ground.

The girls were sisters.   Both were fair,
  But mine was the fairer (so I say).
The dark soon severed us, pair from pair,
  And not long after we lost our way.

We wandered over the country-side,
  And we frightened most of the sheep about,

And I do not think that we greatly tried,

    Having lost our way, to find it out.

The night being fine, it was not worth while.

    We strayed through furrow and corn and grass

We met with many a fence and stile,

    And a quickset hedge, which we failed to pass.

At last we came on a road she knew ;

    She said we were near her father's place.

I heard the steps of the other two,

    And my heart stood still for a moment's space.

Then I pleaded, 'Give me a good-night kiss.'

    I have learned, but I did not know in time,

The fruits that hang on the tree of bliss

    Are not for cravens who will not climb.

We met all four by the farmyard gate,

    We parted laughing, with half a sigh,

And home we went, at a quicker rate,

    A shorter journey, my friend and I.

When we reached the house, it was late enough,
　And many impertinent things were said,
Of time and distance, and such dull stuff,
　But we said little, and went to bed.

We went to bed, but one at least
　Went not to sleep till the black turned grey,
And the sun rose up, and the light increased,
　And the birds awoke to a summer day.

And sometimes now, when the nights are mild,
　And the moon is away, and no stars shine,
I wander out, and I go half-wild,
　To think of the kiss which was not mine.

Let great minds laugh at a grief so small,
　Let small minds laugh at a fool so great.
Kind maidens, pity me, one and all.
　Shy youths, take warning by this my fate.

C

THE CAGED THRUSH

ALAS for the bird who was born to sing!
They have made him a cage; they have clipped his
    wing;
They have shut him up in a dingy street,
And they praise his singing and call it sweet.
But his heart and his song are saddened and filled
With the woods, and the nest he never will build,
And the wild young dawn coming into the tree,
And the mate that never his mate will be.
And day by day, when his notes are heard
They freshen the street—but alas for the bird.

MIDNIGHT

THE air is dark and fragrant
  With memories of a shower,
And sanctified with stillness
  By this most holy hour.

The leaves forget to whisper
  Of soft and secret things,
And every bird is silent,
  With folded eyes and wings.

O blessed hour of midnight,
  Of sleep and of release,
Thou yieldest to the toiler
  The wages of thy peace.

And I, who have not laboured,
Nor borne the heat of noon,
Receive thy tranquil quiet—
An undeservèd boon.

Yes, truly God is gracious,
Who makes His sun to shine
Upon the good and evil,
And idle lives like mine.

Upon the just and unjust
He sends His rain to fall,
And gives this hour of blessing
Freely alike to all.

WHERE'S THE USE

Oh, where's the use of having gifts that can't be
    turned to money?
  And where's the use of singing, when there's no
    one wants to hear?
It may be one or two will say your songs are sweet
    as honey,
  But where's the use of honey, when the loaf of
    bread is dear?

A MAY-DAY MADRIGAL

THE sun shines fair on Tweedside, the river flowing
bright,

Your heart is full of pleasure, your eyes are full of
light,

Your cheeks are like the morning, your pearls are
like the dew,

Or morning and her dew-drops are like your pearls
and you.

Because you are a princess, a princess of the land,

You will not turn your lightsome eyes a moment
where I stand,

A poor unnoticed poet, a-making of his rhymes ;

But I have found a mistress, more fair a thousand
times.

'Tis May, the elfish maiden, the daughter of the
    Spring,

Upon whose birthday morning the birds delight to
    sing.

They would not sing one note for you, if you should
    so command,

Although you are a princess, a princess of the land.

SONG IS NOT DEAD

Song is not dead, although to-day
    Men tell us everything is said.
There yet is something left to say,
    Song is not dead.

While still the evening sky is red,
    While still the morning gold and grey,
While still the autumn leaves are shed,

While still the heart of youth is gay,
    And honour crowns the hoary head,
While men and women love and pray
    Song is not dead.

A SONG OF TRUCE

TILL the tread of marching feet
Through the quiet grass-grown street
Of the little town shall come,
Soldier, rest awhile at home.

While the banners idly hang,
While the bugles do not clang,
While is hushed the clamorous drum,
Soldier, rest awhile at home.

In the breathing-time of Death,
While the sword is in its sheath,
While the cannon's mouth is dumb,
Soldier, rest awhile at home.

Not too long the rest shall be.

Soon enough, to Death and thee,

The assembly call shall come.

Soldier, rest awhile at home.

ONE TEAR

LAST night, when at parting
   Awhile we did stand,
Suddenly starting,
   There fell on my hand

Something that burned it,
   Something that shone
In the moon as I turned it,
   And then it was gone.

One bright stray jewel—
   What made it stray?
Was I cold or cruel,
   At the close of day?

Oh, do not cry, lass !

What is crying worth ?

There is no lass like my lass

In the whole wide earth.

A LOVER'S CONFESSION

WHEN people tell me they have loved
    But once in youth,
I wonder, are they always moved
    To speak the truth?

Not that they wilfully deceive:
    They fondly cherish
A constancy which they would grieve
    To think might perish.

They cherish it until they think
    'Twas always theirs.
So, if the truth they sometimes blink,
    'Tis unawares.

45

Yet unawares, I must profess,
    They do deceive
Themselves, and those who questionless
    Their tale believe.

For I have loved, I freely own,
    A score of times,
And woven, out of love alone,
    A hundred rhymes.

Boys will be fickle.   Yet, when all
    Is said and done,
I was not one whom you could call
    A flirt—not one

Of those who into three or four
    Their hearts divide.
My queens came singly to the door,
    Not side by side.

Each, while she reigned, possessed alone
    My spirit loyal,
Then left an undisputed throne
    To one more royal,

To one more fair in form and face
    Sweeter and stronger,
Who filled the throne with truer grace,
    And filled it longer.

So, love by love, they came and passed,
    These loves of mine,
And each one brighter than the last
    Their lights did shine.

Until—but am I not too free,
    Most courteous stranger,
With secrets which belong to me?
    There is a danger.

Until, I say, the perfect love,
   The last, the best,
Like flame descending from above,
   Kindled my breast,

Kindled my breast like ardent flame,
   With quenchless glow.
I knew not love until it came,
   But now I know.

You smile.   The twenty loves before
   Were each in turn,
You say, the final flame that o'er
   My soul should burn.

Smile on, my friend.   I will not say
   You have no reason ;
But if the love I feel to-day
   Depart, 'tis treason !

If this depart, not once again
    Will I on paper
Declare the loves that waste and wane,
    Like some poor taper.

No, no! This flame, I cannot doubt,
    Despite your laughter,
Will burn till Death shall put it out,
    And may be after.

TRAFALGAR SQUARE

THESE verses have I pilfered like a bee
Out of a letter from my C. C. C.,
   In London, showing what befell him there,
With other things, of interest to me.

One page described a night in open air
He spent last summer in Trafalgar Square,
   With men and women who by want are driven
Thither for lodging, when the nights are fair.

No roof there is between their heads and heaven,
No warmth but what by ragged clothes is given,
   No comfort but the company of those
Who with despair, like them, have vainly striven.

On benches there uneasily they doze,
Snatching brief morsels of a poor repose,
    And if through weariness they might sleep sound,
Their eyes must open almost ere they close.

With even tramp upon the paven ground,
Twice every hour the night patrol comes round
    To clear these wretches off, who may not keep
The miserable couches they have found.

Yet the stern shepherds of the poor black sheep
Will soften when they see a woman weep.
    There was a mother there who strove in vain,
With sobs, to hush a starving child to sleep.

And through the night which took so long to wane,
He saw sad sufferers relieving pain,
    And daughters of iniquity and scorn
Performing deeds which God will not disdain.

There was a girl, forlorn of the forlorn,
Whose dress was white, but draggled, soiled, and torn,
   Who wandered like a ghost without a home.
She spoke to him before the day was born.

She, who all night, when spoken to, was dumb,
Earning dislike from most, abuse from some,
   Now asked the hour, and when he told her 'Two,'
Wailed, 'O my God, will daylight never come?'

Yes, it will come, and change the sky anew
From star-besprinkled black to sunlit blue,
   And bring sweet thoughts and innocent desires
To countless girls.   What will it bring to you?

A SUMMER MORNING

NEVER was sun so bright before,
    No matin of the lark so sweet,
    No grass so green beneath my feet,
Nor with such dewdrops jewelled o'er.

I stand with thee outside the door,
    The air not yet is close with heat,
    And far across the yellowing wheat
The waves are breaking on the shore.

A lovely day! Yet many such,
    Each like to each, this month have passed,
    And none did so supremely shine.
One thing they lacked: the perfect touch
    Of thee—and thou art come at last,
    And half this loveliness is thine.

WELCOME HOME

THE fire burns bright
And the hearth is clean swept,
As she likes it kept,
And the lamp is alight.
She is coming to-night.

The wind's east of late.
When she comes, she'll be cold,
So the big chair is rolled
Close up to the grate,
And I listen and wait.

The shutters are fast,
And the red curtains hide
Every hint of outside.
But hark, how the blast
Whistled then as it passed !

Or was it the train ?
How long shall I stand,
With my watch in my hand,
And listen in vain
For the wheels in the lane?

Hark !   A rumble I hear
(Will the wind not be still ?),
And it comes down the hill,
And it grows on the ear,
And now it is near.

Quick, a fresh log to burn !

Run and open the door,

Hold a lamp out before

To light up the turn,

And bring in the urn.

You are come, then, at last !

O my dear, is it you ?

I can scarce think it true

I am holding you fast,

And sorrow is past.

AN INVITATION

DEAR Ritchie, I am waiting for the signal word to fly,
  And tell me that the visit which has suffered such
    belating
Is to be a thing of now, and no more of by-and-by.
    Dear Ritchie, I am waiting.

The sea is at its bluest, and the Spring is new creating
  The woods and dens we know of, and the fields
    rejoicing lie,
And the air is soft as summer, and the hedge-birds
    all are mating.

The Links are full of larks' nests, and the larks
    possess the sky,
  Like a choir of happy spirits, melodiously debating,
All is ready for your coming, dear Ritchie—yes, and I,
    Dear Ritchie, I am waiting.

FICKLE SUMMER

FICKLE Summer's fled away,
　　Shall we see her face again?
　　Hearken to the weeping rain,
Never sunbeam greets the day.

More inconstant than the May,
　　She cares nothing for our pain,
　　Nor will hear the birds complain
In their bowers that once were gay.

Summer, Summer, come once more,
　　Drive the shadows from the field,
　　　All thy radiance round thee fling,
Be our lady as of yore;
　　Then the earth her fruits shall yield,
　　　Then the morning stars shall sing.

SORROW'S TREACHERY

I MADE a truce last night with Sorrow,
    The queen of tears, the foe of sleep,
To keep her tents until the morrow,
    Nor send such dreams to make me weep.

Before the lusty day was springing,
    Before the tired moon was set,
I dreamed I heard my dead love singing,
    And when I woke my eyes were wet.

THE CROWN OF YEARS

YEARS grow and gather—each a gem
  Lustrous with laughter and with tears,
  And cunning Time a crown of years
Contrives for her who weareth them.

No chance can snatch this diadem,
  It trembles not with hopes or fears,
  It shines before the rose appears,
And when the leaves forsake her stem.

Time sets his jewels one by one.
  Then wherefore mourn the wreaths that lie
  In attic chambers of the past?
They withered ere the day was done.
  This coronal will never die,
  Nor shall you lose it at the last.

HOPE DEFERRED

When the weary night is fled,
And the morning sky is red,
Then my heart doth rise and say,
'Surely she will come to-day.'

In the golden blaze of noon,
'Surely she is coming soon.'
In the twilight, 'Will she come?'
Then my heart with fear is dumb.

When the night wind in the trees
Plays its mournful melodies,
Then I know my trust is vain,
And she will not come again.

THE LIFE OF EARTH

THE life of earth, how full of pain,
  Which greets us on our day of birth,
Nor leaves us while we yet retain
    The life of earth.

There is a shadow on our mirth,
  Our sun is blotted out with rain,
And all our joys are little worth.

Yet oh, when life begins to wane,
  And we must sail the doubtful firth,
How wild the longing to regain
    The life of earth!

GOLDEN DREAM

GOLDEN dream of summer morn,
By a well-remembered stream
In the land where I was born,
Golden dream !

Ripples, by the glancing beam
Lightly kissed in playful scorn,
Meadows moist with sunlit steam.

When I lift my eyelids worn
Like a fair mirage you seem,
In the winter dawn forlorn,
Golden dream !

TEARS

Mourn that which will not come again,
  The joy, the strength of early years.
  Bow down thy head, and let thy tears
Water the grave where hope lies slain.

For tears are like a summer rain,
  To murmur in a mourner's ears,
  To soften all the field of fears,
To moisten valleys parched with pain.

And though thy tears will not awake
  What lies beneath of young or fair
    And sleeps so sound it draws no breath,
Yet, watered thus, the sod may break
  In flowers which sweeten all the air,
    And fill with life the place of death.

64

THE HOUSE OF SLEEP

When we have laid aside our last endeavour,
    And said farewell to one or two that weep,
And issued from the house of life for ever,
    To find a lodging in the house of sleep—

With eyes fast shut, in sunless chambers lying,
    With folded arms unmoved upon the breast,
Beyond the noise of sorrow and of crying,
    Beyond the dread of dreaming, shall we rest?

Or shall there come at last desire of waking,
    To walk again on hillsides that we know,
When sunrise through the cold white mist is breaking,
    Or in the stillness of the after-glow?

Shall there be yearning for the sound of voices,
   The sight of faces, and the touch of hands,
The will that works, the spirit that rejoices,
   The heart that feels, the mind that understands?

Shall dreams and memories crowding from the
     distance,
   Shall ghosts of old ambition or of mirth,
Create for us a shadow of existence,
   A dim reflection of the life of earth?

And being dead, and powerless to recover
   The substance of the show whereon we gaze,
Shall we be likened to the hapless lover,
   Who broods upon the unreturning days?

Not so: for we have known how swift to perish
   Is man's delight when youth and health take wing,
Until the winter leaves him nought to cherish
   But recollections of a vanished spring.

Dream as we may, desire of life shall never

    Disturb our slumbers in the house of sleep.

Yet oh, to think we may not greet for ever

    The one or two that, when we leave them, weep!

THE OUTCAST'S FAREWELL

THE sun is banished,
The daylight vanished,
No rosy traces
   Are left behind.
Here in the meadow
I watch the shadow
Of forms and faces
   Upon your blind.

Through swift transitions,
In new positions,
My eyes still follow
   One shape most fair.

65

My heart delaying
Awhile, is playing
With pleasures hollow,
   Which mock despair.

I feel so lonely,
I long once only
To pass an hour
   With you, O sweet !
To touch your fingers,
Where fragrance lingers
From some rare flower,
   And kiss your feet.

But not this even
To me is given.
Of all sad mortals
   Most sad am I,

Never to meet you,
Never to greet you,
Nor pass your portals
Before I die.

All men scorn me,
Not one will mourn me,
When from their city
I pass away.
Will you to-morrow
Recall with sorrow
Him whom with pity
You saw to-day?

Outcast and lonely,
One thing only
Beyond misgiving
I hold for true,

That, had you known me,
You would have shown me
A life worth living—
    A life for you.

Yes : five years younger
My manhood's hunger
Had you come filling
    With plenty sweet,
My life so nourished,
Had grown and flourished,
Had God been willing
    That we should meet.

How vain to fashion
From dreams and passion
The rich existence
    Which might have been !

Can God's own power
Recall the hour,
Or bridge the distance
That lies between?

Before the morning,
From pain and scorning
I sail death's river
To sleep or hell.
To you is given
The life of heaven.
Farewell for ever,
Farewell, farewell!

YET A LITTLE SLEEP

BESIDE the drowsy streams that creep
　　Within this island of repose,
　　Oh, let us rest from cares and woes,
Oh, let us fold our hands to sleep !

Is it ignoble, then, to keep
　　Awhile from where the rough wind blows,
　　And all is strife, and no man knows
What end awaits him on the deep ?

The voyager may rest awhile,
　　When rest invites, and yet may be
　　　Neither a sluggard nor a craven.
With strength renewed he quits the isle,
　　And putting out again to sea,
　　　Makes sail for his desirèd haven.

LOST LIBERTY

Of our own will we are not free,

   When freedom lies within our power.

   We wait for some decisive hour,

To rise and take our liberty.

Still we delay, content to be

   Imprisoned in our own high tower.

   What is it but a strong-built bower?

Ours are the warders, ours the key.

But we through indolence grow weak.

   Our warders, fed with power so long,

   Become at last our lords indeed.

We vainly threaten, vainly seek

   To move their ruth.   The bars are strong.

   We dash against them till we bleed.

AN AFTERTHOUGHT

You found my life, a poor lame bird
   That had no heart to sing,
You would not speak the magic word
   To give it voice and wing.

Yet sometimes, dreaming of that hour,
   I think, if you had known
How much my life was in your power,
   It might have sung and flown.

TO J. R.

Last Sunday night I read the saddening story
  Of the unanswered love of fair Elaine,
The 'faith unfaithful' and the joyless glory
  Of Lancelot, 'groaning in remorseful pain.'

I thought of all those nights in wintry weather,
  Those Sunday nights that seem not long ago,
When we two read our Poet's words together,
  Till summer warmth within our hearts did glow.

Ah, when shall we renew that bygone pleasure,
  Sit down together at our Merlin's feet,
Drink from one cup the overflowing measure,
  And find, in sharing it, the draught more sweet?

76

That time perchance is far, beyond divining.

   Till then we drain the 'magic cup' apart;

Yet not apart, for hope and memory twining

   Smile upon each, uniting heart to heart.

THE TEMPTED SOUL

Weak soul, by sense still led astray,
  Why wilt thou parley with the foe?
  He seeks to work thine overthrow,
And thou, poor fool! dost point the way.

Hast thou forgotten many a day,
  When thou exulting forth didst go,
  And ere the noon wert lying low,
A broken and defenceless prey?

If thou wouldst live, avoid his face;
  Dwell in the wilderness apart,
    And gather force for vanquishing,
Ere thou returnest to his place.
    Then arm, and with undaunted heart
    Give battle, till he own thee king.

78

YOUTH RENEWED

WHEN one who has wandered out of the way
    Which leads to the hills of joy,
Whose heart has grown both cold and grey,
    Though it be but the heart of a boy—
When such a one turns back his feet
    From the valley of shadow and pain,
Is not the sunshine passing sweet,
    When a man grows young again ?

How gladly he mounts up the steep hillside,
    With strength that is born anew,
And in his veins, like a full springtide,
    The blood streams through and through.

And far above is the summit clear,
   And his heart to be there is fain,
And all too slowly it comes more near
   When a man grows young again.

He breathes the pure sweet mountain breath,
   And it widens all his heart,
And life seems no more kin to death,
   Nor death the better part.
And in tones that are strong and rich and deep
   He sings a grand refrain,
For the soul has awakened from mortal sleep,
   When a man grows young again.

VANITY OF VANITIES

BE ye happy, if ye may,
In the years that pass away.
Ye shall pass and be forgot,
And your place shall know you not.

Other generations rise,
With the same hope in their eyes
That in yours is kindled now,
And the same light on their brow.

They shall see the selfsame sun
That your eyes now gaze upon,
They shall breathe the same sweet air,
And shall reck not who ye were.

Yet they too shall fade at last
In the twilight of the past,
They and you alike shall be
Lost from the world's memory.

Then, while yet ye breathe and live,
Drink the cup that life can give.
Be ye happy, if ye may,
In the years that pass away,

Ere the golden bowl be broken,
Ere ye pass and leave no token,
Ere the silver cord be loosed,
Ere ye turn again to dust.

'And shall this be all,' ye cry,
'But to eat and drink and die?
If no more than this there be,
Vanity of vanity!'

Yea, all things are vanity,
And what else but vain are ye?
Ye who boast yourselves the kings
Over all created things.

Kings! whence came your right to reign?
Ye shall be dethroned again.
Yet for this, your one brief hour,
Wield your mockery of power.

Dupes of Fate, that treads you down
Wear awhile your tinsel crown
Be ye happy, if ye may,
In the years that pass away.

LOVE'S WORSHIP RESTORED

O Love, thine empire is not dead,
Nor will we let thy worship go,
Although thine early flush be fled,
Thine ardent eyes more faintly glow,
And thy light wings be fallen slow
Since when as novices we came
Into the temple of thy name.

Not now with garlands in our hair,
And singing lips, we come to thee.
There is a coldness in the air,
A dulness on the encircling sea,
Which doth not well with songs agree.
And we forget the words we sang
When first to thee our voices rang.

When we recall that magic prime,
We needs must weep its early death.
How pleasant from thy towers the chime
Of bells, and sweet the incense breath
That rose while we, who kept thy faith,
Chanting our creed, and chanting bore
Our offerings to thine altar store!

Now are our voices out of tune,
Our gifts unworthy of thy name.
December frowns, in place of June.
Who smiled when to thy house we came,
We who came leaping, now are lame.
Dull ears and failing eyes are ours,
And who shall lead us to thy towers?

O hark! A sound across the air,
Which tells not of December's cold,
A sound most musical and rare.

Thy bells are ringing as of old,

With silver throats and tongues of gold.

Alas ! it is too sweet for truth,

An empty echo of our youth.

Nay, never echo spake so loud !

It is indeed thy bells that ring.

And lo, against the leaden cloud,

Thy towers ! Once more we leap and spring,

Once more melodiously we sing,

We sing, and in our song forget

That winter lies around us yet.

Oh, what is winter, now we know,

Full surely, thou canst never fail ?

Forgive our weak untrustful woe,

Which deemed thy glowing face grown pale.

We know thee, mighty to prevail.

Doubt and decrepitude depart,

And youth comes back into the heart.

O Love, who turnest frost to flame
With ardent and immortal eyes,
Whose spirit sorrow cannot tame,
Nor time subdue in any wise—
While sun and moon for us shall rise,
Oh, may we in thy service keep
Till in thy faith we fall asleep!

BELOW HER WINDOW

Where she sleeps, no moonlight shines
No pale beam unbidden creeps.
Darkest shade the place enshrines
Where she sleeps.

Like a diamond in the deeps
Of the rich unopened mines
There her lovely rest she keeps.

Though the jealous dark confines
All her beauty, Love's heart leaps.
His unerring thought divines
Where she sleeps.

REQUIEM

FOR thee the birds shall never sing again,

   Nor fresh green leaves come out upon the tree,

The brook shall no more murmur the refrain

      For thee.

Thou liest underneath the windswept lea,

   Thou dreamest not of pleasure or of pain,

Thou dreadest no to-morrow that shall be.

Deep rest is thine, unbroken by the rain,

   Ay, or the thunder. Brother, canst thou see

The tears that night and morning fall in vain

      For thee?

THOU ART QUEEN

Thou art queen to every eye,
 When the fairest maids convene.
Envy's self can not deny
 Thou art queen.

In thy step thy right is seen,
 In thy beauty pure and high,
In thy grace of air and mien.

Thine unworthy vassal I,
 Lay my hands thy hands between ;
Kneeling at thy feet I cry
 Thou art queen !

IN TIME OF DOUBT

'IN the shadow of Thy wings, O Lord of Hosts,
  whom I extol,
  I will put my trust for ever,' so the kingly David
  sings.
'Thou shalt help me, Thou shalt save me, only
  Thou shalt keep me whole,
  In the shadow of Thy wings.'

In our ears this voice triumphant, like a blowing
  trumpet, rings,
  But our hearts have heard another, as of funeral
  bells that toll,
'God of David, where to find Thee?' No reply the
  question brings.

91

Shadows are there overhead, but they are of the
        clouds that roll,
    Blotting out the sun from sight, and overwhelming
        earthly things.
Oh, that we might feel Thy presence!   Surely we
        could rest our soul
            In the shadow of Thy wings.

THE GARDEN OF SIN

I KNOW the garden-close of sin,
  The cloying fruits, the noxious flowers,
  I long have roamed the walks and bowers,
Desiring what no man shall win :

A secret place to shelter in,
  When soon or late the angry powers
  Come down to seek the wretch who cowers,
Expecting judgment to begin.

The pleasure long has passed away
  From flowers and fruit, each hour I dread
  My doom will find me where I lie.
I dare not go, I dare not stay.
  Without the walks, my hope is dead,
  Within them, I myself must die.

URSULA

THERE is a village in a southern land,
By rounded hills closed in on every hand.
The streets slope steeply to the market-square,
Long lines of white-washed houses, clean and fair,
With roofs irregular, and steps of stone
Ascending to the front of every one.
The people swarthy, idle, full of mirth,
Live mostly by the tillage of the earth.

Upon the northern hill-top, looking down,
Like some sequestered saint upon the town,
Stands the great convent.

              On a summer night,
Ten years ago, the moon with rising light

94

Made all the convent towers as clear as day,

While still in deepest shade the village lay.

Both light and shadow with repose were filled,

The village sounds, the convent bells were stilled.

No foot in all the streets was now astir,

And in the convent none kept watch but her

Whom they called Ursula. The moonlight fell

Brightly around her in the lonely cell.

Her eyes were dark, and full of unshed woe,

Like mountain tarns which cannot overflow,

Surcharged with rain, and round about the eyes

Deep rings recorded sleepless nights, and cries

Stifled before their birth. Her brow was pale,

And like a marble temple in a vale

Of cypress trees, shone shadowed by her hair.

So still she was, that had you seen her there,

You might have thought you were beholding death.

Her lips were parted, but if any breath

Came from between them, it were hard to know

By any movement of her breast of snow.

But when the summer night was now far spent,

She kneeled upon the floor.   Her head she leant

Down on the cold stone of the window-seat.

God knows if there were any vital heat

In those pale brows, or if they chilled the stone.

And as she knelt, she made a bitter moan,

With words that issued from a bitter soul,—

'O Mary, Mother, and is this thy goal,

Thy peace   which   waiteth   for   the   world-worn

   heart?

Is it for this I live and die apart

From all that once I knew?   O Holy God,

Is this the blessed chastening of Thy rod,

Which only wounds to heal?   Is this the cross

That I must carry, counting all for loss

Which once was precious in the world to me?

If Thou be God, blot out my memory,

And let me come, forsaking all, to Thee.

But here, though that old world beholds me not,

Here, though I seek Thee through my lonely lot,

Here, though I fast, do penance day by day,

Kneel at Thy feet, and ever watch and pray,

Beloved forms from that forsaken world

Revisit me.   The pale blue smoke is curled

Up from the dwellings of the sons of men.

I see it, and all my heart turns back again

From seeking Thee, to find the forms I love.

'Thou, with Thy saints abiding far above,

What canst Thou know of this, my earthly pain?

They said to me, Thou shalt be born again,

And learn that worldly things are nothing worth,

In that new state.   O God, is this new birth,

Birth of the spirit dying to the flesh?

Are these the living waters which refresh

The thirsty spirit, that it thirst no more?

Still all my life is thirsting to the core.

Thou canst not satisfy, if this be Thou.

And yet I dream, or I remember how,

Before I came here, while I tarried yet

Among the friends they tell me to forget,

I never seemed to seek Thee, but I found

Thou wert in all the loveliness around,

And most of all in hearts that loved me
    well.

'And then I came to seek Thee in this cell,

To crucify my worldliness and pride,

To lay my heart's affections all aside,

As carnal hindrances which held my soul

From hasting unencumbered to her goal.

And all this have I done, or else have striven

To do, obeying the behest of Heaven,

And my reward is bitterness. I seem

To wander always in a feverish dream

On plains where there is only sun and sand,

No rock or tree in all the weary land,

My thirst unquenchable, my heart burnt dry.

And still in my parched throat I faintly
   cry,

Deliver me, O Lord : bow down Thine ear !

' He will not answer me.   He does not hear.

I am alone within the universe.

Oh for a strength of will to rise and curse

God, and defy Him here to strike me dead !

But my heart fails me, and I bow my head,

And cry to Him for mercy, still in vain.

Oh for some sudden agony of pain,

To make such insurrection in my soul
That I might burst all bondage of control,
Be for one moment as the beasts that die,
And pour my life in one blaspheming cry!'

The morning came, and all the convent towers
Were gilt with glory by the golden hours.
But where was Ursula? The sisters came
With quiet footsteps, calling her by name,
But there was none that answered. In her cell,
The glad, illuminating sunshine fell
On form and face, and showed that she was dead.
'May Christ receive her soul!' the sisters said,
And spoke in whispers of her holy life,
And how God's mercy spared her pain and strife,
And gave this quiet death. The face was still,
Like a tired child's, that lies and sleeps its fill.

UNDESIRED REVENGE

Sorrow and sin have worked their will
    For years upon your sovereign face,
    And yet it keeps a faded trace
Of its unequalled beauty still,
    As ruined sanctuaries hold
    A crumbled trace of perfect mould
In shrines which saints no longer fill.

I knew you in your splendid morn,
    Oh, how imperiously sweet !
    I bowed and worshipped at your feet,
And you received my love with scorn.
    Now I scorn you.   It is a change,
    When I consider it, how strange
That you, not I, should be forlorn.

Do you suppose I have no pain
To see you play this sorry part,
With faded face and broken heart,
And life lived utterly in vain?
Oh would to God that you once more
Might scorn me as you did of yore,
And I might worship you again !

POETS

CHILDREN of earth are we,
Lovers of land and sea,
Of hill, of brook, of tree,
  Of all things fair;
Of all things dark or bright,
Born of the day and night,
Red rose and lily white
  And dusky hair.

Yet not alone from earth
Do we derive our birth.
What were our singing worth
  Were this the whole?
Somewhere from heaven afar
Hath dropped a fiery star,
Which makes us what we are,
  Which is our soul.

A PRESENTIMENT

It seems a little word to say—
    Farewell—but may it not, when said,
    Be like the kiss we give the dead,
Before they pass the doors for aye?

Who knows if, on some after day,
    Your lips shall utter in its stead
    A welcome, and the broken thread
Be joined again, the selfsame way?

The word is said, I turn to go,
    But on the threshold seem to hear
    A sound as of a passing bell,
Tolling monotonous and slow,
    Which strikes despair upon my ear,
    And says it is a last farewell.

A BIRTHDAY GIFT

No gift I bring but worship, and the love
    Which all must bear to lovely souls and pure,
    Those lights, that, when all else is dark, endure ;
Stars in the night, to lift our eyes above ;

To lift our eyes and hearts, and make us move
    Less doubtful, though our journey be obscure,
    Less fearful of its ending, being sure
That they watch over us, where 'er we rove.

And though my gift itself have little worth,
    Yet worth it gains from her to whom 'tis given,
    As a weak flower gets colour from the sun.
Or rather, as when angels walk the earth,
    All things they look on take the look of heaven—
    For of those blessed angels thou art one.

CYCLAMEN

I HAD a plant which would not thrive,
　　Although I watered it with care,
　　I could not save the blossoms fair,
Nor even keep the leaves alive.

I strove till it was vain to strive.
　　I gave it light, I gave it air,
　　I sought from skill and counsel rare
The means to make it yet survive.

A lady sent it me, to prove
　　She held my friendship in esteem ;
　　I would not have it as she said,
I wanted it to be for love ;
　　And now not even friends we seem,
　　And now the cyclamen is dead.

LOVE RECALLED IN SLEEP

THERE was a time when in your face
  There dwelt such power, and in your smile
I know not what of magic grace;
  They held me captive for a while.

Ah, then I listened for your voice!
  Like music every word did fall,
Making the hearts of men rejoice,
  And mine rejoiced the most of all.

At sight of you, my soul took flame.
  But now, alas! the spell is fled.
Is it that you are not the same,
  Or only that my love is dead?

I know not—but last night I dreamed
   That you were walking by my side,
And sweet, as once you were, you seemed,
   And all my heart was glorified.

Your head against my shoulder lay,
   And round your waist my arm was pressed,
And as we walked a well-known way,
   Love was between us both confessed.

But when with dawn I woke from sleep,
   And slow came back the unlovely truth,
I wept, as an old man might weep
   For the lost paradise of youth.

FOOTSTEPS IN THE STREET

Oh, will the footsteps never be done?
> The insolent feet
> Thronging the street,
Forsaken now of the only one.

The only one out of all the throng,
> Whose footfall I knew,
> And could tell it so true,
That I leapt to see as she passed along,

As she passed along with her beautiful face,
> Which knew full well
> Though it did not tell,
That I was there in the window-space.

109

Now my sense is never so clear.

It cheats my heart,

Making me start

A thousand times, when she is not near.

When she is not near, but so far away,

I could not come

To the place of her home,

Though I travelled and sought for a month and a day.

Do you wonder then if I wish the street

Were grown with grass,

And no foot might pass

Till she treads it again with her sacred feet?

FOR A PRESENT OF ROSES

CRIMSON and cream and white—
　My room is a garden of roses !
Centre and left and right,
　Three several splendid posies.

As the sender is, they are sweet,
　These lovely gifts of your sending,
With the stifling summer heat
　Their delicate fragrance blending.

What more can my heart desire ?
　Has it lost the power to be grateful ?
Is it only a burnt-out fire,
　Whose ashes are dull and hateful ?

Yet still to itself it doth say,

'I should have loved far better

To have found, coming in to-day,

The merest scrap of a letter.'

IN TIME OF SORROW

DESPAIR is in the suns that shine,
  And in the rains that fall,
This sad forsaken soul of mine
  Is weary of them all.

They fall and shine on alien streets
  From those I love and know.
I cannot hear amid the heats
  The North Sea's freshening flow

The people hurry up and down,
  Like ghosts that cannot lie ;
And wandering through the phantom town
  The weariest ghost am I.

H

A NEW SONG TO AN OLD TUNE

FROM VICTOR HUGO

IF a pleasant lawn there grow
By the showers caressed,
Where in all the seasons blow
Flowers gaily dressed,
Where by handfuls one may win
Lilies, woodbine, jessamine,
I will make a path therein
For thy feet to rest.

If there live in honour's sway
An all-loving breast
Whose devotion cannot stray,
Never gloom-oppressed—

If this noble breast still wake
For a worthy motive's sake,
There a pillow I will make
    For thy head to rest.

If there be a dream of love,
    Dream that God has blest,
Yielding daily treasure-trove
    Of delightful zest,
With the scent of roses filled,
With the soul's communion thrilled,
There, oh ! there a nest I 'll build
    For thy heart to rest.

THE FIDDLER

There's a fiddler in the street,
   And the children all are dancing:
Two dozen lightsome feet
   Springing and prancing.

Pleasure he gives to you,
   Dance then, and spare not!
For the poor fiddler's due,
   Know not and care not.

While you are prancing,
   Let the fiddler play.
When you're tired of dancing
   He may go away.

THE FIRST MEETING

LAST night for the first time, O Heart's Delight,
　　I held your hand a moment in my own,
　　The dearest moment which my soul has known,
Since I beheld and loved you at first sight.

I left you, and I wandered in the night,
　　Under the rain, beside the ocean's moan.
　　All was black dark, but in the north alone
There was a glimmer of the Northern Light.

My heart was singing like a happy bird,
　　Glad of the present, and from forethought free,
Save for one note amid its music heard :
　　God grant, whatever end of this may be,
That when the tale is told, the final word
　　May be of peace and benison to thee.

A CRITICISM OF CRITICS

How often have the critics, trained
   To look upon the sky
Through telescopes securely chained,
   Forgot the naked eye.

Within the compass of their glass
   Each smallest star they knew,
And not a meteor could pass
   But they were looking through.

When a new planet shed its rays
   Beyond their field of vision,
And simple folk ran out to gaze,
   They laughed in high derision.

They railed upon the senseless throng
Who cheered the brave new light.
And yet the learned men were wrong,
The simple folk were right.

MY LADY

My Lady of all ladies!   Queen by right
  Of tender beauty ; full of gentle moods ;
  With eyes that look divine beatitudes,
Large eyes illumined with her spirit's light ;

Lips that are lovely both by sound and sight,
  Breathing such music as the dove, which broods
  Within the dark and silence of the woods,
Croons to the mate that is her heart's delight.

Where is a line, in cloud or wave or hill,
  To match the curve which rounds her soft-flushed
    cheek ?
  A colour, in the sky of morn or of even,
To match that flush ?   Ah, let me now be still !
  If of her spirit I should strive to speak,
    I should come short, as earth comes short of
    heaven.

PARTNERSHIP IN FAME

Love, when the present is become the past,
  And dust has covered all that now is new,
  When many a fame has faded out of view,
And many a later fame is fading fast—

If then these songs of mine might hope to last,
  Which sing most sweetly when they sing of you,
  Though queen and empress wore oblivion's hue,
Your loveliness would not be overcast.

Now, while the present stays with you and me,
  In love's copartnery our hearts combine,
    Life's loss and gain in equal shares to take.
Partners in fame our memories then would be:
  Your name remembered for my songs; and mine
    Still unforgotten for your sweetness' sake.

A CHRISTMAS FANCY

EARLY on Christmas Day,
Love, as awake I lay,
And heard the Christmas bells ring sweet and clearly,
My heart stole through the gloom
Into your silent room,
And whispered to your heart, ' I love you dearly.'

There, in the dark profound,
Your heart was sleeping sound,
And dreaming some fair dream of summer weather.
At my heart's word it woke,
And, ere the morning broke,
They sang a Christmas carol both together.

Glory to God on high !
Stars of the morning sky,

Sing as ye sang upon the first creation,

When all the Sons of God

Shouted for joy abroad,

And earth was laid upon a sure foundation.

Glory to God again!

Peace and goodwill to men,

And kindly feeling all the wide world over,

Where friends with joy and mirth

Meet round the Christmas hearth,

Or dreams of home the solitary rover.

Glory to God! True hearts,

Lo, now the dark departs,

And morning on the snow-clad hills grows grey.

Oh, may love's dawning light

Kindled from loveless night,

Shine more and more unto the perfect day!

THE BURIAL OF WILLIAM
THE CONQUEROR

OH, who may this dead warrior be
 That to his grave they bring?
'Tis William, Duke of Normandy,
 The conqueror and king.

Across the sea, with fire and sword,
 The English crown he won;
The lawless Scots they owned him lord,
 But now his rule is done.

A king should die from length of years,
 A conqueror in the field,
A king amid his people's tears,
 A conqueror on his shield.

But he, who ruled by sword and flame,
Who swore to ravage France,
Like some poor serf without a name,
Has died by mere mischance.

To Caen now he comes to sleep,
The minster bells they toll,
A solemn sound it is and deep,
May God receive his soul !

With priests that chant a wailing hymn,
He slowly comes this way,
To where the painted windows dim
The lively light of day.

He enters in. The townsfolk stand
In reverent silence round,
To see the lord of all the land
Take house in narrow ground.

While, in the dwelling-place he seeks,
    To lay him they prepare,
One Asselin FitzArthur speaks,
    And bids the priests forbear.

'The ground whereon this abbey stands
    Is mine,' he cries, 'by right.
'Twas wrested from my father's hands
    By lawlessness and might.

Duke William took the land away,
    To build this minster high.
Bury the robber where ye may,
    But here he shall not lie.'

The holy brethren bid him cease;
    But he will not be stilled,
And soon the house of God's own peace
    With noise and strife is filled.

And some cry shame on Asselin,
    Such tumult to excite,
Some say, it was Duke William's sin,
    And Asselin does right.

But he round whom their quarrels keep,
    Lies still and takes no heed.
No strife can mar a dead man's sleep,
    And this is rest indeed.

Now Asselin at length is won
    The land's full price to take,
And let the burial rites go on,
    And so a peace they make.

When Harold, king of Englishmen,
    Was killed in Senlac fight,
Duke William would not yield him then
    A Christian grave or rite.

Because he fought for keeping free
His kingdom and his throne,
No Christian rite nor grave had he
In land that was his own.

And just it is, this Duke unkind,
Now he has come to die,
In plundered land should hardly find
Sufficient space to lie.

THE DEATH OF WILLIAM RUFUS

THE Red King's gone a-hunting, in the woods his
  father made
For the tall red deer to wander through the thicket
  and the glade,
The King and Walter Tyrrel, Prince Henry and
  the rest
Are all gone out upon the sport the Red King loves
  the best.

Last night, when they were feasting in the royal
  banquet-hall,
De Breteuil told a dream he had, that evil would
  befall

I

If the King should go to-morrow to the hunting of
the deer,
And while he spoke, the fiery face grew well-nigh
pale to hear.

He drank until the fire came back, and all his heart
was brave,
Then bade them keep such woman's tales to tell an
English slave,
For he would hunt to-morrow, though a thousand
dreams foretold
All the sorrow and the mischief De Breteuil's brain
could hold.

So the Red King's gone a-hunting, for all that they
could do,
And an arrow in the greenwood made De Breteuil's
dream come true.

They said 'twas Walter Tyrrel, and so it may have
    been,
But there's many walk the forest when the leaves are
    thick and green.

There's many walk the forest, who would gladly see
    the sport,
When the King goes out a-hunting with the nobles
    of his court,
And when the nobles scatter, and the King is left
    alone,
There are thickets where an English slave might
    string his bow unknown.

The forest laws are cruel, and the time is hard as
    steel
To English slaves, trod down and bruised beneath
    the Norman heel.

Like worms they writhe, but by-and-by the Norman
   heel may learn
There are worms that carry poison, and that are not
   slow to turn.

The lords came back, by one and two, from straying
   far apart,
And they found the Red King lying with an arrow in
   his heart.
Who should have done the deed, but him by whom
   it first was seen?
So they said 'twas Walter Tyrrel, and so it may have
   been.

They cried upon Prince Henry, the brother of the
   King,
And he came up the greenwood, and rode into the
   ring.

He looked upon his brother's face, and then he
 turned away,
And galloped off to Winchester, where all the
 treasure lay.

'God strike me,' cried De Breteuil, 'but brothers'
 blood is thin !
And why should ours be thicker that are neither kith
 nor kin ? '
They spurred their horses in the flank, and swiftly
 thence they passed,
But Walter Tyrrel lingered and forsook his liege the
 last.

They say it was enchantment, that fixed him to the
 scene,
To look upon his traitor's work, and so it may have
 been.

But presently he got to horse, and took the seaward
way,
And all alone within the glade, in state the Red
King lay.

Then a creaking cart came slowly, which a charcoal-
burner drove.
He found the dead man lying, a ghastly treasure-
trove ;
He raised the corpse for charity, and on his wagon
laid,
And so the Red King drove in state from out the
forest glade.

His hair was like a yellow flame about the bloated
face,
The blood had stained his tunic from the fatal arrow-
place.

Not good to look upon was he, in life, nor yet when
    dead.
The driver of the cart drove on, and never turned
    his head.

When next the nobles throng at night the royal
    banquet-hall,
Another King will rule the feast, the drinking and
    the brawl,
While Walter Tyrrel walks alone upon the Norman
    shore,
And the Red King in the forest will chase the deer
    no more.

AFTER WATERLOO

On the field of Waterloo we made Napoleon rue
  That ever out of Elba he decided for to come,
For we finished him that day, and he had to run
    away,
    And yield himself to Maitland on the Billy-ruffi-
    um.

'Twas a stubborn fight, no doubt, and the fortune
    wheeled about,
    And the brave Mossoos kept coming most un-
    comfortable near,
And says Wellington the hero, as his hopes went
    down to zero,
    'I wish to God that Blooker or the night was
    only here!'

But Blooker came at length, and we broke Napoleon's
    strength,
  And the flower of his army—that's the old
    Imperial Guard—
They made a final sally, but they found they could
    not rally,
  And at last they broke and fled, after fighting
    bitter hard.

Now Napoleon he had thought, when a British ship
    he sought,
  And gave himself uncalled-for, in a manner, you
    might say,
He'd be treated like a king with the best of every
    thing,
  And maybe have a palace for to live in every
    day.

He was treated very well, as became a noble swell,
  But we couldn't leave him loose, not in Europe
  anywhere,
For we knew he would be making some gigantic
  undertaking,
  While the trustful British lion was reposing in
  his lair.

We tried him once before near the European shore,
  Having planted him in Elba, where he promised
  to remain,
But when he saw his chance, why, he bolted off to
  France,
  And he made a lot of trouble—but it wouldn't
  do again.

Says the Prince to him, 'You know, far away you'll
  have to go,
  To a pleasant little island off the coast of Africay,

Where they tell me that the view of the ocean deep
    and blue,
  Is remarkable extensive, and it's there you'll have
    to stay.'

So Napoleon wiped his eye, and he wished the Prince
    good-bye,
  And being stony-broke, made the best of it he
    could,
And they kept him snugly pensioned, where his
    Royal Highness mentioned,
  And Napoleon Boneyparty is provided for for
    good.

Now of that I don't complain, but I ask and ask in
    vain,
  Why me, a British soldier, as has lost a useful
    arm

Through fighting of the foe, when the trumpets
    ceased to blow,
    Should be forced to feed the pigs on a little
        Surrey farm,

While him as fought with us, and created such a
    fuss,
    And in the whole of Europe did a mighty deal
        of harm,
Should be kept upon a rock, like a precious fighting
    cock,
    And be found in beer and baccy, which would
        suit me to a charm?

DEATH AT THE WINDOW

THIS morning, while we sat in talk
  Of spring and apple-bloom,
Lo ! Death stood in the garden walk,
  And peered into the room.

Your back was turned, you did not see
  The shadow that he made.
He bent his head and looked at me ;
  It made my soul afraid.

The words I had begun to speak
  Fell broken in the air.
You saw the pallor of my cheek,
  And turned—but none was there.

He came as sudden as a thought,

    And so departed too.

What made him leave his task unwrought?

    It was the sight of you.

Though Death but seldom turns aside

    From those he means to take,

He would not yet our hearts divide,

    For love and pity's sake.

MAKE-BELIEVES

When I was young and well and glad,
I used to play at being sad;
Now youth and health are fled away,
At being glad I sometimes play.

A COINCIDENCE

EVERY critic in the town
Runs the minor poet down;
Every critic—don't you know it?
Is himself a minor poet.

ART'S DISCIPLINE

Long since I came into the school of Art,
A child in works, but not a child in heart.
Slowly I learn, by her instruction mild,
To be in works a man, in heart a child.

THE TRUE LIBERAL

THE truest Liberal is he
Who sees the man in each degree,
Who merit in a churl can prize,
And baseness in an earl despise,
Yet censures baseness in a churl,
And dares find merit in an earl.

A LATE GOOD NIGHT

My lamp is out, my task is done,
    And up the stair with lingering feet
I climb.   The staircase clock strikes one.
    Good night, my love! good night, my sweet!

My solitary room I gain.
    A single star makes incomplete
The blackness of the window pane.
    Good night, my love! good night, my sweet!

Dim and more dim its sparkle grows,
    And ere my head the pillows meet,
My lids are fain themselves to close.
    Good night, my love! good night, my sweet!

My lips no other words can say,

But still they murmur and repeat

To you, who slumber far away,

Good night, my love! good night, my sweet!

AN EXILE'S SONG

My soul is like a prisoned lark,
   That sings and dreams of liberty,
The nights are long, the days are dark,
   Away from home, away from thee!

My only joy is in my dreams,
   When I thy loving face can see.
How dreary the awakening seems,
   Away from home, away from thee!

At dawn I hasten to the shore,
   To gaze across the sparkling sea—
The sea is bright to me no more,
   Which parts me from my home and thee.

At twilight, when the air grows chill,
   And cold and leaden is the sea,
My tears like bitter dews distil,
   Away from home, away from thee.

I could not live, did I not know
   That thou art ever true to me,
I could not bear a doubtful woe,
   Away from home, away from thee.

I could not live, did I not hear
   A voice that sings the day to be,
When hitherward a ship shall steer,
   To bear me back to home and thee.

Oh, when at last that day shall break
   In sunshine on the dancing sea,
It will be brighter for the sake
   Of my return to home and thee !

FOR SCOTLAND

Beyond the Cheviots and the Tweed,
   Beyond the Firth of Forth,
My memory returns at speed
   To Scotland and the North.

    For still I keep, and ever shall,
      A warm place in my heart for Scotland,
    Scotland, Scotland,
      A warm place in my heart for Scotland.

Oh, cruel off St. Andrew's Bay
   The winds are wont to blow!
They either rest or gently play,
   When there in dreams I go.

And there I wander, young again,
        With limbs that do not tire,
Along the coast to Kittock's Den,
        With whinbloom all afire.

I climb the Spindle Rock, and lie
        And take my doubtful ease,
Between the ocean and the sky,
        Derided by the breeze.

Where coloured mushrooms thickly grow,
        Like flowers of brittle stalk,
To haunted Magus Muir I go,
        By Lady Catherine's Walk.

In dreams the year I linger through,
        In that familiar town,
Where all the youth I ever knew,
        Burned up and flickered down.

There 's not a rock that fronts the sea,

    There 's not an inland grove,

But has a tale to tell to me

    Of friendship or of love.

    And so I keep, and ever shall,

        The best place in my heart for Scotland,

    Scotland, Scotland,

        The best place in my heart for Scotland !

THE HAUNTED CHAMBER

LIFE is a house where many chambers be,
   And all the doors will yield to him who tries,
   Save one, whereof men say, behind it lies
The haunting secret.   He who keeps the key,

Keeps it securely, smiles perchance to see
   The eager hands stretched out to clutch the prize,
   Or looks with pity in the yearning eyes,
And is half moved to let the secret free.

And truly some at every hour pass through,
   Pass through, and tread upon that solemn floor,
     Yet come not back to tell what they have found.
We will not importune, as others do,
   With tears and cries, the keeper of the door,
     But wait till our appointed hour comes round.

NIGHTFALL

LET me sleep.   The day is past,
　And the folded shadows keep
Weary mortals safe and fast.
　　Let me sleep.

I am all too tired to weep
　For the sunlight of the Past
Sunk within the drowning deep.

Treasured vanities I cast
　In an unregarded heap.
Time has given rest at last.
　　Let me sleep.

IN TIME OF SICKNESS

Lost Youth, come back again!
Laugh at weariness and pain.
Come not in dreams, but come in truth,
Lost Youth.

Sweetheart of long ago,
Why do you haunt me so?
Were you not glad to part,
Sweetheart?

Still Death, that draws so near,
Is it hope you bring, or fear?
Is it only case of breath,
Still Death?

BY THE SAME AUTHOR

The Scarlet Gown: being Verses by a St. Andrews Man (R. F. MURRAY). Small 8vo, 120 pp., elegantly bound in cloth, ... **2s. 6d.**

'Full of sparkle and point and drollery. . . . The "Song from the Princess" is capital.' **Saturday Review.**

'The imitation from Wordsworth is particularly "fetching," as also "The Waster's Presentiment." "Vivien's Song" is worth quoting.' **Athenæum.**

'Nothing could be better than some of his stanzas on the bore.' **Literary World.**

'When he is humorous, he is unquestionably successful. "The City of Golf," "A Street Corner," "An Imitation of Wordsworth" are particularly good.' **Spectator.**

A. M. HOLDEN : 23 PATERNOSTER ROW